ZAK BLUE

AND THE GREAT SPACE CHASE

Dr. Bo Wagner

Word of His Mouth Publishers
Mooresboro, NC

ISBN: 978-1-941039-00-7
Printed in the United States of America
©2016 Dr. Bo Wagner (Robert Arthur Wagner)

Word of His Mouth Publishers
Mooresboro, NC 28114

704-477-5439
www.wordofhismouth.com

Cover art by Megan Morrison at
Littlebittycreativity.com

CHAPTER ONE

To say that Zak Blue was a handful would be an understatement. He was self-centered, arrogant, egotistical, rebellious, dishonest, and impetuous. And it is that last quality, his impetuosity, that was causing him his current trouble.

"Blee gana offrey intaglia!"

Zak kept looking straight ahead, though he had taken note of every whispered word he had just heard.

"Yes, I know there are guards everywhere. It's almost like there's an escaped convict on the loose that they expect to try and steal one of their precious spaceships."

He said those words with a sardonic chuckle, knowing that they were true and that he himself was the recently, albeit involuntarily, emancipated prisoner. Beside him, his best (perhaps it would be more accurate to say "only") friend Deragon turned an inquisitive face toward him and then shook his round, scaly head back and forth at this latest example of Zak Blue's rashness.

"Oyt canna gian bana lithas tereas hunda?"

"No, D, I couldn't have been patient three months. I was patient enough NOT to escape the day they brought me in. I was patient enough to wait two full weeks to check out of the very sparse confines of our local government's finest involuntary confinement. I think that is more than enough patience for one lifetime. Three months? Out of the question, friend, out of the question.

Zak puffed a blonde curl out from in front of his left eye. He would have to get a haircut at some point; that head of wavy golden curls was as good as a neon sign to everyone looking for him. His picture would soon be floating across every suspended screen in half a dozen galaxies, along with a hefty reward posted just below his face.

Deragon was right, of course. He may be a short, orange, scaly, cold-blooded, half-human half-reptile, but his reasoning was unassailable. If Zak had just stayed put for a while, he would have been released (again), placed on probation (again), forced to undergo "character re-establishment classes" (yes, again), and then he would have been able to go about life as he was supposed to know it.

But therein was the problem; Zak Blue was not interested in life as he was supposed to know it. He had an untamed spirit the size of the Milky Way and enough pent-up energy to power the Balindrome itself. He simply could not settle down into a monotonous, humdrum, societally efficient life. His parents (may they rest in peace) had known this by the time he was three years old when he dismantled the government-issued nutrition robot his family was assigned. He rebuilt it in such a way that it actually produced palatable food like pancakes and grilled cheese sandwiches instead of the bland, tasteless, yet highly nutritious vegobars each human on Earth was now expected to consume.

That brought Zak's first (but certainly not last) visit from the Planetary Efficiency Team, P.E.T. for short. His parents were mortified and promised that they would watch their little genius much more carefully to ensure that he did not demonstrate anymore "non-conformist behavior."

That promise proved impossible to keep. Zak Blue had an I.Q. that put even interplanetary computerized organisms to shame and no inner restraints to keep that intelligence in check. He built personal air pods that were faster than inner atmosphere speed limits. He had the entire east sector's trash sent to city hall with the touch of a button. And then he sky-posted a picture of the mayor at home in his Incredible Hulk pajamas...

Getting the picture was easy enough. Every suspended screen is both a viewer and a two-way communication tool. Hacking into them and using them to snap pictures of people was supposed to be impossible but had taken all of about three and a half minutes for Zak. That the mayor was dressed in pajamas depicting a two-hundred-year-old superhero from ancient comic books was an unexpected yet highly entertaining bonus. But when Zak Blue sky posted that picture for all of Devadare City to see, he had become target number one for those in authority. That began a series of confrontations, many of which were, in fact, his fault, but quite a few of which were not.

Two weeks shy of his seventeenth birthday and knowing that he was now officially in a world of trouble, Zak knew that the welcome mat for him here on Earth was rolled up and tucked away forever.

"I had to get out, D, I can't spend my life mourning for the past, and I certainly can't allow myself to be squished into a boring, boxy mold. These authority types are as much fun as unflavored oatmeal. Anyway, it isn't like we have much holding us here."

"Oyt shada tealk hefa tafalare."

"Thank you for that impromptu sermon, Pope Pumpernickel. Yes, I know I shouldn't have stolen that transmuter. I figured that out when I got arrested yet again, thus necessitating my escape. But if I hadn't stolen the transmuter, I wouldn't have been able to perfect my portable slide drive."

"Oyt hypera lova et gi telesopa!"

"I better *hope* it is perfected? What does hope have to do with anything? Facts are facts. I am a human, you are a Tarq, water is wet, and my inventions always work."

He hoped.

Because if it didn't, three months in local confinement would seem like a walk in the park. He knew that his escape alone was good for two years, yet he had been willing to risk that rather than waste three months in lockup. And once he took that spaceship, he could count on twenty years if he was ever caught.

He could not afford a single mistake.

CHAPTER TWO

As Deragon and Zak peered around the corner at the longed-for ship surrounded by all of the guards, they were both, in their minds, sizing up the task at hand. Two of them. One ship. At least thirty guards.

The Balindrome hangar itself was massive, the largest structure on Earth. Twenty miles long, forty miles wide, five miles high. The walls and ceiling and floors on every level were sheets of pure energy. There were more than five thousand ships inside its confines. The energy walls protected everything and everyone inside from such mundane things as rain, snow, and wind, and also from more hostile things like Peragonian cannons raining destruction down from the sky. After the attack of 2123 devastated half of the space vessels on Earth, steps had been taken to ensure that such a thing would never be possible again.

"Lina gi oya skema?"

"Well, first, we need some kind of a distraction. Then we need to get into that ship as quickly as possible and get it out of one of the ports without getting killed. From there, we fly, really fast, and hope for the best."

Deragon looked at Zak with bewilderment.

"Hefa gi et?"

"Yes, that's it. Do you have a better idea?

The Tarq shook his head at that and spent the next half-minute emitting a series of vibrations and whistles that Zak could not understand but was quite sure meant that Deragon was either very upset or laughing at him.

Truthfully, he could not blame him. Genius or no, there was really not much in the way of good odds that they could ever pull this off. Working from the outer edge of their problem, even if they got a ship out into space, they would be followed by enforcement cruisers that could surely catch them. That particular problem, Zak was certain he could overcome. His slide drive could be installed in three minutes, tops, and should give any decent ship a good chance at outrunning any pursuit. If they got a really good ship, it would outrun pursuit by a long way.

Working inward, though, there was also the problem of the exo-ring around the planet. Generated by power harnessed from the sun, it would keep any ship from making it to orbit unless it had electronic clearance from The

Innerspace Authority below. That part could be beaten if the ship could be passed the exo-ring in less than forty-seven seconds. A good pilot could not do it. A great pilot could. Zak knew he was a great pilot.

Further in still was the Balindrome itself. Every ship was surrounded by at least thirty guards, each one with neural disruptor guns. That presented a fate worse than death. If he were shot with one of those, he would lay on the ground in no pain at all, fully awake yet unable to move a muscle. The guards would then calmly call for the authorities from P.E.T. They would, equally calmly, mosey on over and pick him up like a sack of trash, haul him to prison, drop him in a deep dark cell, and then, and only then, would he be undisrupted. He would then spend a very, very long time regretting his actions.

"We have to get that ship, D, we have to. The snifferbots are probably already closing in on us, and this old-fashioned cover scent won't hold out forever. One ship. Couldn't they at least have left one single ship unguarded? Would that be too much to ask?"

There are those moments when an idea hits you, an idea so outlandish and at the same time so perfect that it just takes your breath away. From the wild-eyed look that came across Zak's face and the way he gasped, Deragon knew this was one of those times. He knew it, and he also knew that it always meant trouble.

"There is one ship like that, D; there is one ship that won't be guarded..."

"Ona! Ona! Cerito onat!"

"Yes, yes, absolutely yes," Zak countered.

"Da Valcona Celesto cannea ba airo."

"It can be flown, D, it has been done before."

The Falcon Wing was both a prototype and an anachronism. In the earliest days of flight, mankind had used hand-eye coordination rather than computers and electronics. Even on up into the twenty-first century, pilots had used hand controls in conjunction with electronics to fly. A good pilot was able to react even quicker than a computer was and was able to handle crafts going two and three thousand miles per hour. But with the advent of orbital spacecraft and then deep space travel crafts, everything had changed. After multiple deaths of pilots who could never react quick enough to danger at very near the speed of light, the Thought Interface was born.

In short, pilots no longer used any type of hand controls to pilot a craft. Every pilot was mentally synched with his ship, and the Thought Interface allowed him to react on the deepest of mental levels with the heart of the craft itself. In essence, the pilot became a part of the ship, and vice-versa. This revolutionary technology had almost completely done away with any form of "old fashioned" piloting of inner-atmosphere or outer-space ships. When I say "almost completely," what I really mean is "all but one man and all but one ship."

"I still have his poster on my wall back home, or back at what used to be home."

Davian De-Saad was an old-fashioned daredevil and a hero to Zak and other kids like him. Early on, he had rebelled against the notion of the Thought Interface, arguing that it had atrophied any real skills and abilities on the part of pilots. Normally, a person like that would have been summarily arrested for non-conformity, but since his father was high up in government, he had often been given a pass on his "indiscretions."

And then came Falcon Wing. Davian De-Saad had somehow managed to pull off the unthinkable. Not only did he secretly build the fastest spacecraft of its day, but he did so without any Thought Interface. The hand controls were still there. Yes, the computer could certainly plot in a course and then pilot itself when at warp speeds or higher just for convenience, but the pilot could at any time take the controls himself without being overridden. Such a thing was unthinkable and regarded as completely impossible to handle. But Davian De-Saad did it. He launched it, beat the closing exo-shield, and jumped to hyperspace.

He should have come back a hero, but instead, he never made it back alive.

"Davian gi thana, Zak."

"Yes, I know he is dead. It was a fool's errand for even a pilot as great as him to try and navigate the Leonid Expulsion."

The quaver rays had pierced the ship, not leaving so much as a trace of damage to it. Davian, though, flesh and blood and neural synapsis, was not so fortunate. It would have been a million to one odds of dodging each and every one at that speed until he could make it through safely, and it only took one to kill him.

The ship had drifted for days before being picked up by a salvage cruiser and brought back to earth. Davian was given a respectable burial with plenty of pomp and circumstance. But he also became a lesson in every child's education tablet. His life had encouraged individuality and risk-taking, but in his death, he became a monument to conformity. Every child was taught to fear doing things on his own; to do things on one's own brought danger and death. It was far better to trust the authorities and to stay in line. That lesson was taught so well, so graphically, so "let's show Davian's dead body to each child at least a thousand times," that the Falcon Wing became more feared than if it had been Dante's Inferno.

Which is why it was sitting right there, five levels up, all by itself, unguarded.

CHAPTER THREE

At P.E.T. headquarters, General Loopjeister was pacing like a caged lion.

"Why hasn't he been caught yet?"

"He will be soon, General; I assure you. The snifferbots have tracked his scent right to the Balindrome, just as you suspected, him and his fish-faced friend."

Loopjeister just glared at the small, whiny voiced, groveling underling and his report. He was angry; coldly, furiously angry. Zak Blue was making things inefficient, and his superiors did not like it when things were inefficient. And when they were unhappy, they made him unhappy.

He did not like being unhappy.

"Double the pursuit. Re-verify that every ship is guarded. Send officers to interview every relative, friend, enemy, and pet the boy has ever had."

Simperson groveled again and said with an even more nasally tone than before, "Yes, my leader. Consider almost all of it done."

"Almost? ALMOST?!?"

"He has no family, sir. His parents both died ten years ago. The boy grew up in Villagecare."

"I don't care if he is Little Orphan Annie re-incarnated; he will get no sympathy from me. FIND HIM, YOU WORTHLESS FOOL!"

Simperson nearly tripped all over himself running from the room to fulfill the order, angry over being verbally abused yet again.

As he rushed down the hallway, he reflected on the situation. A groveling underling he may be, but he was surely smarter than everyone thought. He was, in fact, more in tune with this situation than all of his superiors, including General Loopjeister.

"They will not catch him," he muttered to himself. "The boy is as daring as De-Saad himself and far more intelligent. Still, what can he do? Every ship is guarded by dozens of soldiers; he can never get off of this planet."

Suddenly he stopped. There was a ship. One ship. One ship that would not be guarded at all.

The little man turned to rush back into the control center but immediately stopped. Fool? How dare the General call him a fool, yet again, in front of everyone. Yet, this was a common occurrence. Everyone in the upper echelons of P.E.T. was smug, condescending, and abrasive.

And Simperson tended to forever be the butt of their jokes and their vitriol.

Why then should he betray Zak Blue to them?

Their paths had crossed only once, three years ago, at a Character Re-establishment Class...

"Terry," Zak had said as he put both hands on the little man's shoulders, "you are a better man than these people think you are."

Simperson never forgot that. In a world obsessed with perfection and yet seemingly incapable of realizing just how far short they were falling, one supposedly bad apple had said the only kind thing to him he could ever remember from anyone.

And so the little man turned back around and walked calmly down the corridor. He would do as he was told, nothing less, but nothing more.

Back in the Balindrome, Zak and Deragon were now just outside the hanger on level five. The snifferbots were closing in, they knew that, but they also knew they had at least a couple more minutes. If they were being chased by real live dogs, they would doubtless be caught by now. But, as so often was the case, modern man was too clever by half. The snifferbots had been programmed not just to smell, but also to calculate probabilities based on the information given them. And, since that information doubtless included the fact that no one could fly the Falcon Wing, Zak and Deragon were being blessed by a very precious, albeit very small window of opportunity.

There was no shooting, no mad dash to the ship. The shooting and the mad dash would doubtless begin once the Falcon Wing roared to life. For the time being, after taking a couple of deep breaths to calm themselves, Zak and Deragon simply stepped out into the open and casually walked toward the prize. No hurrying, no sudden or erratic movements, the anomaly detectors would have immediately alerted to such things.

Thirty feet. Twenty. Ten. Five. A step onto the gangplank, then another, then another.

When their feet cleared the opening, everything changed.

Zak bolted for the cockpit, Deragon for the shield generator. Seven seconds later, the engines roared to life. One second after that, the inner space shield enveloped the Falcon Wing, unseen, yet the only thing that would stand between them and death. Two seconds after that, the first blaster bolts hit the shield and were harmlessly absorbed, though they now began to come by the dozens as soldiers rushed toward the ship. Three seconds after that, the ship rose twenty feet, turned upward at a seventy-degree angle, and shot like a bullet out of a gun through the hanger opening.

Four seconds later, an alarm sounded in the control room. Then two seconds of hesitation by a man at the monitor who could not believe what he was seeing.

That two-second delay would prove to be the difference between life and death.

Forty-seven seconds would have been the window to beat, but anyone good at math can see that between the four seconds to the alarm and the two seconds of a delay before the man in the control room slapped the button to close the exo-shield, they now had a generous fifty-three seconds to get through.

It was enough, by exactly one second.

As the exo-shield slammed shut behind them, Zak literally dove out of the cockpit, and Deragon vaulted in to take his place, shouting unintelligibly. Zak ran like never before, nearly diving head first into the warp drive chamber. Across the ship's communication channel, Zak could hear Deragon screaming for him to hurry; the enforcement cruisers were closing in.

Frantically Zak ripped the portable slide drive out of his flight pack. Not even bothering to gently remove the cover, he simply yanked the top off of the warp drive housing. Back home, in his simulator, he had been able to install the slide drive on absolutely any vessel in three minutes or less. He hoped he could do the same in reality.

Suddenly the ship lurched and rocked, and Zak knew they were being fired on. That was not good, not good at all. Deragon's frantic, high-pitched warbles confirmed his fear; the enforcement cruisers were apparently much faster than they expected.

His fingers flew. There was no thought; there was no time for it. There was only clawing instinct as he worked faster than even he had ever imagined possible.

Two minutes and fourteen seconds, done.

Zak rushed back for the cockpit; Deragon vaulted into the co-pilot seat; Zak vaulted into the pilot seat.

"Falcon Wing," the mechanical voice came across the com, "prepare to be taken."

"Not today," Zak whispered in anger, "not ever."

And with a slap of the blue button to his right, the Falcon Wing was, in less than a second, more than seven million miles away.

CHAPTER FOUR

Most people are familiar with faster than the speed of light travel, otherwise known as warp drive. I suppose we can all thank *Star Trek* for that. But man will never be satisfied with any set speed. No matter how fast he can go, he will always seek out a way to go just a tiny bit faster.

And that is where the slide drive came in.

As a child, Zak had a grasp of warp drive that most adults never achieved. But, for lack of a simpler way to explain it, warp drive is all about "push." And in a way, that made it no more advanced than when ancient American Indians paddled down a creek in a canoe made of bark. Zak had somehow always known that if you could manage to add "pull" to the mix, you would go faster.

The slide drive was an engineering marvel. So much so, that he had received a failing grade when he turned in a paper trying to explain it since his "expert" teachers all agreed that it was utterly unfeasible. Better still, it was no bigger than an old paperback book. Yet, when Zak fused it into the warp drive, the Falcon Wing, unbeknownst to his pursuers, suddenly became the fastest ship in the known universe. Not by much, but certainly by enough. Between the push and the pull, which, if it could have been seen by the eye would have looked something like a treadmill loop of pure energy, the Falcon Wing was now seven or eight percent faster than the fastest ships ever known and had been blazing across the universe for seven hours since her escape.

But that did not mean they were out of the woods, not by a long shot.

Unlike cheesy sci-fi movies, the cold hard fact about warp speed travel is as follows: the faster you go, the sooner you must stop. No ship and no shield can endure the unfathomable strain of that kind of speed indefinitely, not even in the cold vacuum of outer space. What that means on a practical level, as in when one is being chased, is that whoever has the fastest ship could get to a point quicker than others. But whoever has the biggest ship and the best shields could conceivably close the gap by maintaining warp speed just a bit longer than whoever they were chasing.

Thus, at some point, a pursued ship would either have to find a way to disappear or would have to get some kind of a barrier between itself and any pursuer. The good news is, whoever was being chased, though they could be tracked, could choose the time and place they dropped out of hyperspace.

Zak knew they were being pursued. The flashing red lights, beeping warning signals, and images on the Celsius screen left no doubt of that.

"We're pulling away, D, but we won't be able to get totally out of range before we have to go back to sub-warp speed. I count seven cruisers back of us. That's more than I want to fight by about, let's see, seven."

"Blee gi mas mala lise."

"More bad news is the last thing I need!"

"Blee gana mas, tereas centrok, aptem ut lasa weldo nafa."

Zak checked the forescreen and, sure enough, the Tarq was right. There were three full squadrons from outlying posts moving to cut them off.

That just didn't make any sense! It was just one unusable ship, and he was just one runaway kid. There was no reason for P.E.T. to move heaven and earth to come after him like this. A cruiser or two, sure, but seven back of him and three squadrons ahead? That he could never have anticipated. When Gerwain McCuen had assassinated Regent Wan Lee, P.E.T. had only sent five cruisers to apprehend him. Zak was being pursued like he was a greater criminal than a notorious murderer by a factor of five!

"This doesn't make any sense, D. Who in the world has enough pull to over-react like this?"

The answer really was irrelevant, at least for now. But Zak had the sneaky feeling that at some point it would be very relevant indeed.

"Whoever they are, they've done their math very well and very quickly. If we take this puppy as far as she will go, we'll be dropping out of hyperspace right into their hands. Speed isn't going to get us out of this, at least not for now. We need a way to put a brick wall between them and us, something they can't follow us through."

"Ona! Ona!"

"Can you think of a better idea?"

"Ewet gopha tha aptem!"

"Then we die trying!" Zak shouted back furiously. "Real death would be preferable to what waits for us if we get caught. I will NOT be caught, not alive, anyway. If you want to go that route, just hit the escape pod, pal; I won't try to stop you. But if you choose to stay here, shut your orange mouth and buckle up. Dead or alive, we are going through the Leonid Expulsion."

Deragon knew it was suicide. But, true friend that he was, and lover of freedom just as fiercely as Zak, he immediately fell silent. He would live with his best friend, or he would die with him, but he would not abandon him. Not now, not ever.

Zak knew the odds too, and they were bleak. There was no possibility of escape at this point without navigating the Expulsion. There were also about a million to one odds of actually being able to navigate it successfully. Davian had died trying, and he was probably going to end up

24

dead as well, along with the only real friend he had ever known.

For whatever reason, that thought brought a heavy weight of sadness to Zak. Dying himself he could live with (irony, that), but being the cause of Deragon's death was almost enough to bring him to a point he never allowed himself to go to, the point of tears.

But why should it be that way? Was he not a loner, a rebel, a selfish narcissist? Those were, in fact, the very words written in red on his psych evaluation from his very earliest days in Villagecare. That, and a snide note that he was a "loser with little to no socially redeeming value."

But musing on the past would not fix the present, and Zak was not one for long reverie anyway. He had survived his childhood by burning all of the feelings out of his heart, cauterizing his emotions, obliterating his concern. He would survive, or he would die, but he would be free either way.

But he could not win unless he lived, and Zak wanted to win, very badly. It had been that way ever since the "loser" tag was slapped on him. From that very moment, Zak Blue was obsessed with winning, no matter what the game or the stakes.

"I am going to cut it thinner than a razor's edge, D. I am going to drop us out of hyperspace so close to the edge of the Expulsion that they cannot so much as get a single shot at us. But that means we are going to have to do what even Davian would not have dreamed of. Going into it at that speed is an even bigger fool's game than what he tried. But if we get through it, it will be days before the cruisers can circle it, and by that time, we will be very, very long gone."

The Leonid Expulsion could not be seen with the naked eye, nor could the quaver rays that it emits. But, in a twist of irony, old-fashioned night vision goggles did what even modern sensors could not do: they allowed a person to see the rays flashing at them. Not that this was necessarily a help; it simply allowed a person to see what was going to kill him. For anyone to actually navigate it would be nothing short of a miracle.

What would it take?

Several things, actually. A ton (or five) of luck, a small ship, nimble controls, and a pilot with hand-eye coordination that was very literally instinctive to the point of being felt as much as it was seen. It could not be thought about, it could not be planned, it could only be as though a person's soul was doing the piloting rather than his mind or his hands.

Zak knew he was instinctive, primal, but was he enough so? The difference between "yes" and "no" would either be a monument or a grave stone.

CHAPTER FIVE

When Falcon Wing dropped out of hyperspace, it was not a jaw-dropping moment; it was a jaw-dropping split-second. Instantly, right in front of a line of cruisers skirting along it, the small ship (though I suppose the term small is relative; in square footage, it was about the size of an old 747 Jumbo Jet, though sleek and exquisite in shape and design) plunged into the abyss itself, the Leonid Expulsion.

Commander Cannonade could not believe his eyes; his brain simply refused for a moment to register what had just happened. Slowly, he tapped the side of his temple and activated his implanted com device.

"P.E.T. command, this is Commander Cannonade of Enforcement Cruiser Alpha Dog."

"Go ahead, Alpha Dog."

"We won't be bringing in your fugitive, at least not for several days, and definitely not alive. We tracked him and boxed him in between the Leonid and us, just as you instructed, but he did not pull up short and surrender. He plunged into it at just barely sub-warp speed. By now, he's as dead as the old Aztec Empire. Do you want us to make our way around and pick him up, or should we just let the Falcon Wing drift out of memory this time? Please advise."

"Stand by, Alpha Dog."

Commander Cannonade slowly shook his head as he waited in silence. Who was this one kid that was important enough for all of this attention? And why would anyone give themselves up to certain death rather than be taken back to Earth to face what would surely be fairly mild judgment, all things considered?

"Alpha Dog, stand by, P.E.T. is channeling a message through to you, a message from Planetary Command."

Cannonade's heart literally skipped a beat, and his head jerked back visibly as if he had been struck. In thirty years of being in the military, twenty of which had been in command of his own squadron, never once had he been contacted by the secretive and pretty much all powerful Planetary Command. Nations had ceased to be generations ago and national governments along with them. The only government most people ever had any contact with or information from was P.E.T. But P.E.T. was merely the shadow of the beast. Planetary Command ruled, well, everything and everyone. It was never seen or heard from directly, but everyone knew it was there.

Currently, Prime Minister Tiller Mansen was the man at the top of the food chain, the unquestioned leader of the Planetary Command. And it was his face that now hovered in front of Commander Cannonade, his voice that spoke low and threateningly, so much so as if he were actually there in person.

"Commander Cannonade, this is Prime Minister Mansen. I will give you sixty seconds to either be at top speed, making your way around what the boy fool has dashed into or those same sixty seconds to be following him into it. You may choose which of those two options you follow, but I assure you, there is no third option. The clock starts now. If it reaches zero and you are not on one of those two paths, I will remotely detonate your ship with you and everyone else on it."

And with that, the communication stopped, the face disappeared, every jaw on the bridge dropped, and every eye got as wide as saucers.

"Move!" Cannonade shouted at his chief officer. "Get us to top speed, and do it now! Set us a course around the Expulsion. Go, go, go!"

As the ship's engines roared to life, everyone else in the squadron followed suit. This made no sense at all, no sense to anyone. But what made even less sense was the thought of dying rather than doing as one was told.

In the Expulsion, Zak and Deragon were not making a sound. They really were not even thinking. Deragon was gripping the sides of the co-pilot seat so hard that they were being deformed under the pressure. He was sweating, which is something that those of the Tarq species simply never do. His head was plastered back against the seat.

Zak was simply reacting. The quaver rays were coming so fast and furious that his Adam's apple was up in his throat and nearly cutting off his breathing. Every movement of his hands was tiny, at no point did he move the controls more than one thirty-second of an inch in any direction. If they were going to survive, he would have to go in the straightest line possible. It would be sort of like piloting through a giant tube and only moving a few feet in any direction as you did. Now picture all of that at speeds just short of hyperdrive, which would be the speed necessary to get them through and gone before the pursuit could catch up enough to track them.

In short, it was impossible to survive.

Yet Zak was no ordinary teenager and no ordinary pilot. Everything was utterly primal; he and the ship were doing a concerted space flight ballet, weaving, bobbing, dipping, rising, slowing, jerking ahead, rolling at angles, taking the concept of a roller coaster to extremes that a twenty-first-century human would never have been able to imagine.

Seven minutes and twenty-one seconds in, he passed Davian De Saad's mark. The only expression he gave was a muted grunt. He could not afford to lose focus.

At the twenty-minute mark, he was soaked to the bone with sweat, and his body was trembling. All except for his hands; those he was willing to be as smooth as a surgeon's stroke.

At thirty-seven minutes a quaver ray came right through the ship and just barely grazed the hair on the right side of his head. That was close; way, way too close.

At forty-one minutes, he began to lose feeling in the lower half of his body, and he felt like he was going to throw up.

At forty-four minutes and seventeen seconds, the Falcon Wing burst through the other side of the Leonid Expulsion and back out into open space. Zak Blue had done the impossible; he had done what no one else would ever be able to do again.

And at forty-four minutes and nineteen seconds, Zak Blue passed out cold and slid out of the pilot seat and down into the floor.

CHAPTER SIX

Cold. Wet. Those were the first two thoughts that slowly wiggled their way into his re-emerging consciousness. Zak blinked a couple of times and saw soothing lights overhead. He reached a trembling hand up to his forehead and felt the source of the cold and wet, a rag that was laying just above his eyes. He was in the infirmary.

Ever so slowly he rolled onto one side, put a trembling arm out, and pushed up. He swung his feet down onto the floor, gently, oh so gently. Then he fell off of the bed, onto his knees, and threw up.

Seconds later Deragon was there, chirping and warbling at him, scolding him. He picked his friend up and laid him back in bed, propping a pillow behind his head. He wiped his face with another wet rag, disintegrated what Zak had just left on the floor, then shook his head and grinned.

"Oyt eimi odda."

Zak softly laughed. The Tarq was right: most likely, he was insane. But he was alive; they both were.

"How long have I been out, D?"

"Uhna yomoo."

"Feels like way more than an hour. Of course, it also feels like I could use another week or two."

Deragon warbled low and slow, shaking his head.

"What? What is it?"

He was not going to like the answer. It meant that he did not have a few weeks, or even a few days, really not even a few hours to rest.

Deragon spoke to the communication center of the ship, and Falcon Wing responded by projecting a hologram of a message. A very personal message for Zak Blue, from Tiller Mansen himself.

"Well, well, young man, apparently you have managed to do the impossible; otherwise, you would not be activating this message. Congratulations. I am sure you must know who I am. Are you surprised to hear from me? After all, you are just a boy, and the crime you have committed is merely the theft of one small piece of technology and one useless ship. Do you wonder why such a trivial matter should even register with Planetary Command? Do you wish that we would just look the other way and let you finally be free?

"If that is what you wish, then I am going to make you very unhappy. You have no idea why, and I do not feel the need to enlighten you, I am simply going to tell you to listen to me very carefully: you will never be free. I will make it my personal mission in life to drag you back to Earth in chains. I will move every asset at my disposal to hunt you down from planet to planet, solar system to solar system, galaxy to galaxy, quadrant to quadrant, dimension to dimension.

"You will never be allowed to sleep, never be allowed to rest, never be allowed to breathe easily. As of this moment I have nothing else to do but find you. And if I have nothing else to do but find you, then no one else has anything else to do, either.

"You and I will be seeing each other again very soon, Zak Blue, I promise."

The image disappeared, and Deragon dropped his eyes toward the floor. This was bad, very bad. He wondered how Zak would take all of this. But when he cut his eyes upward to see what was written on his friend's face, he did not see the fear that he expected. Zak Blue had his brow wrinkled, his mouth twisted to the side, and his eyes were loaded with question.

"He said 'again,' D."

Deragon's eyes got wide like saucers. How had he missed that, and what could it mean? One thing was for sure, it could not be good at all.

CHAPTER SEVEN

The universe lay before them. It's kind of funny, really, but Zak had never given much thought to what would come next. Actually, he had given it no thought at all. His entire focus had been to escape Earth and never come back. But he had made no plans at all about where to go and what to do.

For the time being, they were intent on getting space, and a lot of it, between them and their pursuers.

From time to time Zak spoke the command and watched as a holographic mirror appeared in front of him. He would turn his head slightly to the left and stare at the thin, snow white streak that now ran down the side of his curly blond head. It was about the width of a pencil and ran from his temple toward the back of his head. That quaver ray came about an eighth of an inch from killing him.

Falcon Wing was at top speed, and Zak planned on keeping her there as long as possible. He had also cloaked the ship, masked the trail, and was flying an unorthodox course. He and the ship had plotted and were taking a trail that led through event horizons, around asteroid belts, incredibly close to supernovas, anything and everything to throw off pursuit, or at least to slow it down. He had no idea why he was being chased, but it didn't really matter. The universe is incomprehensibly huge, no one could exhaust it in a thousand lifetimes, and if he had to, he would go to the very ends of it to avoid ever seeing Earth again. Did they want a great space chase? Fine, he would give it to them.

It did gnaw at him, though. Why were they chasing him? Why had Prime Minister Mansen said he would see him "again?" Any ordinary fugitive would not have cared, but Zak did care because he was very far from ordinary. His genius brain could not lightly lay aside a riddle wrapped in an enigma like that. He knew that, even while he was physically running as far away from it as he could, his brain would be tinkering with it, toying with it, trying to unravel it.

In the meantime, Zak and Deragon had something very precious; a massive head start. Zak knew that it would take the pursuit days to get around the Expulsion, and by that time, the trail would have dissipated and spread so far and wide as to be almost impossible to follow. Yes, they would chase him. Yes, they would have every known outpost in the universe on alert for him. No, even with all of their resources, he would not be easy to catch with that big of a lead on them.

"Especially not if we can find someplace to hole up for a while and let the trail go completely cold on them."

"Lina?"

"Sorry, just thinking out loud. There are billions and billions of habitable planets and moons out there. If we can get to one and shut down for a while, the waves of the universe will wipe out any trace of our passing just like waves lapping up onto a beach wash away footprints. D, we need to hide Falcon Wing, and us, for that matter, for a while."

"Ajij gopha ewet sajay?"

"Well, a really wise philosopher from the twentieth century used to talk about being 'intentionally random.' In this case, I think that is the wisest thing we can do. Planetary Command will be running probability scenarios to determine where we will go. But if we remove all symmetry and logic from the equation, they will, by being rational, send themselves on a wild goose chase because of our irrationality."

The Tarq, bewildered, shook his head and put his hands on the side of his face. Trying to follow Zak Blue's logic was like trying to predict the path of a rabid Earth squirrel that had been injected with sugar.

With a wave of the hand, Zak yanked a 4-D hologram of the Beta Quadrant into view, and it filled the entire bridge of the ship. All sight of seats and control panels disappeared, and it was as if Zak and Deragon were giants standing in the middle of space. Suddenly, with another wave of his hand, all of the stars and non-habitable planets and moons were gone. That still left billions of little dots of lights. One more wave of the hand and everything started spinning.

Deragon had trouble standing up, both of his stomachs were doing flips. Somehow, though, Zak was standing like a statue in the middle of it all, face tilted upward, arms outstretched, laughing with excitement.

"Pick one, D, pick any of them!"

But Deragon was in no shape to pick anything. This time, he was the one on the floor throwing up. Zak laughed again, practically intoxicated by the size and scope and beauty of the heavenly bodies whizzing around him in such pattern and perfection. Faster it all came, faster, faster, faster, till all of the lights were practically blending and blurring together, when, finally, Zak pointed and shouted one word:

"There!"

And everything came to a stop.

Slowly the lights of the cabin reappeared, and all of the planets and moons faded from view except the one that Zak now held in his outstretched right hand. Deragon was disintegrating the second mess for the day and this time was wiping his own face with a wet rag.

"What do you know about Velaronas Four?" Zak asked as he turned the holographic sphere over and back in his hand.

Deragon just looked up at him and shook his head, the universal sign for "nothing, nothing at all."

"Excellent. Neither do I. No known human foot or Earth probe has ever been there, and it is so far off of the beaten path that it would take a crazy man to ever go there. It's perfect.

"Falcon Wing, set a course, top speed. D, kick back and relax. Between the time we can be at warp speed and the times we will have to let Falcon Wing slow and cool, we have two months to rest, eat, and play Calla Ball.

"Velaronas Four, here we come. Let's hope you are hospitable. And let's hope that Prime Minister Mansen gets a bad case of the screaming jeebies trying to figure out where we've gone."

CHAPTER EIGHT

Time passes slowly on a small ship in outer space. Try to imagine two months of riding in a vehicle down country roads without passing any towns and without stopping. That will give you some sense of the boredom that Zak and Deragon were feeling.

They had already rested so much that the very thought of any more rest made them tired. They played hundreds of games of Calla Ball, which provided them ample opportunity to argue and fuss and fight. They took careful notes of each and every heavenly body that they passed near. That part of their time would doubtless prove valuablc to them at some point in their fugitive wanderings. Whoever knew the most about the terrain had a distinct advantage.

The good part about the two months heading toward Velaronas Four is that they were incredibly successful in throwing off pursuit. They were, at the moment, fifteen minutes from their intended stop and completely lost to all of Planetary Command. They had no way of knowing that, of course, but Zak had a pretty good hunch.

"I believe we can breathe pretty easy for now, D. There has not been a hint or a whiff of any pursuit, nor has there been any activity ahead of us indicating that anyone knows that we are headed this way. Planetary Command may be big and powerful, but every resource they have is still tiny compared to the universe they have to search. Let's hope Velaronas Four is a tropical vacation paradise. If it is, we may just settle down forever."

Deragon warbled his approval of that concept. Maybe there would be some palm trees. Ever since arriving on Earth as a tiny Tarq, he had loved fresh coconut juice. It tasted good, and it gave his orange skin a silky appearance. Who knows, maybe there would even be a future Mrs. Deragon on this new world to comment on how nice his skin looked as he drank that coconut jui—

"Captain Blue, First Officer Deragon, please, help me. Come quickly, it may be too late otherwise."

Zak and Deragon both literally jumped out of their chairs as if they had been shocked by a cattle prod. The voice was coming across the ship's com and was steady yet urgent.

It was also lovely. Incredibly, musically, melodiously lovely. And for some reason, whether it was the sheer loveliness of the voice or the fact that it had broken up two months of semi-silent boredom, both of our intrepid fugitives missed what should have been a glaring, neon-sign kind of fact: the voice had addressed them both by name.

Oh, and also the fact that without the assistance of the universal translator, both of them heard the voice in their own language.

Zak quickly snatched up the handpiece for the com device. It honestly was not necessary for him to do so; he could have just spoken, and the ship would have heard it and communicated it just as well. But somehow Zak always felt more comfortable actually speaking into it while holding it, a lot like the ancients would have done with their now antiquated smartphones.

"Velaronas Four, this is Captain Zak Blue of the Falcon Wing. Who are you, where are you, and what is your emergency?"

"This is Andromeda Tellecraft, daughter of King Tellecraft, ruler of this world. I am in the mountains at the headwaters of the Mingyani River. My position is secure at the moment but surrounded. Please come to heading 66457 by 38421. There is room for you to land and a pathway between two peaks that will get you to my location safely. Hurry, Captain Blue, I don't know how long -"

And the communication stopped.

"Andromeda? Come in Andromeda. Come in Andromeda!"

"Lina gi sajay epi?"

"I don't know, D, but we need to get there, and fast. She sounds like she is really in trouble."

Zak launched himself into the captain's chair, grasped the controls, and urged Falcon Wing forward. And at no point did it occur to him that he, a wanted fugitive, was rushing into an unknown danger that could very well blow his cover and result in him being carried back to Earth in shackles.

Andromeda Tellecraft was not really Andromeda Tellecraft, nor was she the daughter of a king. But she did need help, and she smiled as she saw the Falcon Wing coming. Zak Blue had wasted no time in rushing to the location she had provided for him.

The ship made a graceful arc through the lower atmosphere, parting the purple clouds majestically. A few seconds later and she was down, her landing thrusters whining to a stop.

In the cockpit, Zak and Deragon were anxious. Someone needed help, but they knew that they did not know what dangers awaited them out on the surface.

"Sensors indicate perfectly breathable atmosphere. D, let's get down to the armory and suit up. If there is an attack coming Andromeda's way, and ours, I want to be ready."

Deragon nodded, and together they made their way down to the lower level, into the armory, and were quickly preparing themselves for whatever they might face. Once they were satisfied by their energarmor and their choice of weaponry, they made for the ship's gangplank, and Zak barked one final order as they disembarked.

"Falcon Wing, once we are out, go to full cloak and full shields and hover at thirty feet. I do not want anyone to see or touch you. Do not respond to anyone or anything other than Deragon or me."

"Yes sir, Captain," Falcon Wing responded. Her voice was smooth and businesslike, and Zak knew that she would do exactly as he had instructed. He had spent a good bit of time over the two months of travel programming her to recognize him as her captain and become a virtual extension of himself.

If he were going to survive out here in the wild universe, he would have to be able to trust his ship, and she would have to be able to trust him.

CHAPTER NINE

A tap of a button on the energarmor bracelets on their wrists. That is all it took for both of the newcomers to Velaronas Four to be sheathed in a just barely visible body armor. They secured their weapons to their sides and backs and quickly assumed a rather professional two o'clock/eight o'clock formation. They moved quietly, quickly, and their eyes were always moving as they drank in every rock, hill, contour, plant, and unidentifiable object.

Andromeda was watching.

From her position, she saw them coming up through the pass. Zak had, though, much to her chagrin, landed the Falcon Wing just beyond her field of view. No matter. He was clearly being cautious, but that could be changed. A flip of the hair, a seductive laugh, a sly glance of the eyes, and this Earth creature would be eating from her hands, as would the Tarq. A bit of a complication, that there were two of them, but not anything she could not handle. Both of them would think that she had eyes and affections only for him.

Zak and Deragon kept moving. Just as if they had been trained for this for life, they made no sound and missed no detail. Zak especially, with his incredible IQ and nearly photographic memory, could have closed his eyes and recounted every minute detail of every step they had just taken.

"A bit closer, come, come, come, just a little more," Andromeda whispered.

Overhead there were three moons showing in the daytime sky, and two suns. One sun was roughly the size and proximity of Earth's sun to Earth and the other about half the size but slightly closer. The atmosphere was not heavy, but it was composed in such a way that even with the two suns it did not feel in the least bit uncomfortable. In fact, it was a bit cool if anything. There was a breeze, but it was an odd one. It was much more like undulating waves rather than a steady stream.

The terrain, at least where they were, was rocky and arid, much like the old Arizona desert before the artificial water pods irrigated it into a veritable garden.

Onward and upward they came, drawing nearer and nearer to the cave where Andromeda was waiting. And at just the right moment, she stepped out of the cave and into view.

Zak gasped. She was as beautiful as her voice. Five foot five. Thin as a wisp. Hair as black as a raven. Flawlessly smooth skin. Eyes so blue they made Zak's look dull by comparison. She smiled, and his heart skipped a beat.

As did Deragon's. He could not believe the vision of beauty he was seeing. Four foot three. Green scales, as silky as a Terranian Hydropod. Perfectly round mouth. Thin tail swishing gracefully behind her. Eyes as green as a sunset over the Pleiadon. Oh yes, this was most definitely the future Mrs. Deragon.

"This is way too easy," she said under her breath.

"Welcome to Velaronas Four, Captain Blue and First Officer Deragon. You have my eternal gratitude for coming to my aid. Please, come in."

And with that, she turned gracefully and made her way back into the cave.

Zak and Deragon followed, no longer caring to even notice the terrain, or the sky, or the scenery...

Miles away, across the valley and up on the side of another mountain, another person was watching. Watching, though, would not be quite the right word. Deragon and Zak and Andromeda were very far out of sight of her physical eyes. But just as Andromeda had known they were coming, so did she. Her powers were not quite as strong as Andromeda's, therefore, she was unable to break through and contact them first. But they were strong, very strong, and in many ways much more dangerous.

"I think not, not this time. I have a few new things up my sleeve, dearie, things I do not believe you and your new friends will see coming."

And with that, she too turned and walked gracefully into her cave. Tonight belonged to her adversary, but tomorrow was another day. Another day indeed...

CHAPTER TEN

The fire gave off a pinkish hue and a pleasant warmth. Zak and Deragon were sipping either coffee or blendling, depending on which one you asked. Andromeda was gracefully swishing around the cave, bringing snacks and in general being the perfect hostess. And all the while, she was telling her story and answering their questions.

"It started about five years ago. Things had been peaceful in the kingdom for as many generations as history could record. But then an enemy came from the east. No one really knows who she is, but her armies soon ravaged these lands. My father, King Tellecraft, fought valiantly, as did all of his armies. But, alas, the sorceress and her forces were too strong. My father was killed, his armies scattered, and I only barely escaped into the hills with my life.

"There are still many who are loyal to me, and they send me word each chance they get of

53

all that is happening in the kingdom. They rally to defend me when I am attacked, but that is all they are able to do, they are certainly not powerful enough to mount a successful offensive. My father's armies, what is left of them, long for the day that the sorceress can be defeated, and I can be enthroned as the rightful ruler of this world."

Zak nodded in understanding. He recalled many things like this from Earth's own history. How many times had a peaceful people been subjugated by a stronger enemy? There would always be a Napoleon, a Hitler, an Alexander the Great, a Genghis Khan, individuals who believed that might made right.

"You said that your position was secure but surrounded, but I did not notice any sign of forces on our way down or in."

She smiled, and gratitude beamed out of her as she did.

"That is correct, my hero. As they saw your ship coming this way, they vanished into the valley. Even without firing the first shot, you have already begun to turn the tide. But rest assured that will not be enough. The evil ones gathered against me have run, but not for long and not far. They will doubtless come back and in far greater numbers."

And then the girl calling herself Andromeda Tellecraft began to cry; first softly, and then in a torrent. Zak and Deragon rushed to either side of her, Zak grabbing her by her smooth right forearm, and Deragon by her scaly left forearm. They helped her to a chair, and shushed and cooed over her as her heaving sobs finally began to subside.

"I am sorry, so very, very sorry to have brought you here. No one should have to die but me. Please, go back to your ship and leave me before it is too late."

"We're not going anywhere; your trouble is now our trouble, and we will be here until things are safe for you," Zak said as Deragon nodded in agreement. Deragon, for his part, had two emotions running side by side through him. Pity for this victimized beauty and growing admiration for his friend Zak. He would honestly never have guessed that Zak would be this kind to a Tarq that he had never met. Maybe his selfish friend was finally starting to grow up.

"I cannot ask you to face such danger for me, for I do not know how to win this war. What possible tactic can turn three individuals in a defensive posture into victors against such an overwhelming force?"

Zak smiled. As a child, while others were reading comics, he was absorbing the works of the greatest military minds of Earth's history; Sun Tzu, Robert E. Lee, Norman Schwarzkopf, Dontavius Brown, and Vadren Powers.

"And why should we accept the premise of fighting from a defensive posture? Vadren Powers said 'the only thing keeping a defensive force on defense is the expectation that that is how it should be. When in the majority, attack. When in the minority, forget you are in the minority, and attack anyway. If you forget that you are in the minority, your enemy will quickly forget that he is in the majority.' "

Andromeda looked shocked, positively shocked at that idea. Her eyes grew wide, pleading, and she looked as if she would faint.

"You cannot! There are only two of you. You do not have enough weapons to survive an assault against the eastern foe."

"My dear Andromeda," Zak said as he stretched his arms behind his head, interlocking his fingers and flexing his biceps while pretending not to do so, "we have more at our disposal than you think. Your fear has made you forgetful, as fear often does to those who are not fighters. We have the one thing that, according to my sensors, no one in this world has. We have a spaceship, and by the standards of this planet, she is heavily weaponized. The Falcon Wing can be the deciding factor in all of this, I assure you."

Andromeda's eyes grew wide again, and she put her hand over her mouth as in shock. Then she spoke from behind it. "Falcon Wing! That thought had never occurred to me. How very wise you are! How would you use her to win this battle?"

This was, really, going far better than she could have imagined. These two were like putty in her hands; she was shaping them and molding them into the very toys she needed to accomplish her purpose. Soon Castella would be gone, just a smoking pile of rubble, and she would own this world alone, it would be her personal playground. She could predict exactly what would happen next: Zak Blue would ask for the coordinates of her enemy, then he would quickly rush back to his ship, fly fifteen minutes across the valley, unload a barrage of energon blasts, and reduce Castella to rubble right there in her cave. It was as easy to predict as the rising of the suns.

But, despite her ability to read minds, she really did not know what she was dealing with when it came to Zak Blue. If she were able to really read him as deeply as she could read others, she would have known that the only thing predictable about him was that he was utterly unpredictable.

Imagine her surprise, then, and Deragon's, when he said, "It won't be hard at all. Falcon Wing has the weaponry to make quick work of whoever or whatever this world can throw at us. That being the case, we really don't have to be in any big rush. We will get a good night's sleep, then early tomorrow morning D and I will take a little scouting trip. We will set out on foot, check everything very carefully, and then by tomorrow night, we will be right back here. Then the morning after that we will use Falcon Wing to decimate every target that needs hitting. By late that afternoon, we will be flying you into the capital city, and you will have the coronation that the daughter of a king deserves."

Andromeda, for the very first time, was utterly speechless. She started to stutter and stammer, but Zak cut her off.

"No, no, there is no need to thank us. You just get a good night's sleep. I will set up a hovering mini sentry outside the cave, and if anything comes within a thousand yards, we will know about it. D and I can curl up in the back of the cave. Trust me, after growing up in Villagecare, it will seem like a luxury suite."

Immediately they set to work. Zak walked out of the cave a few feet, reached into his tool belt, and pulled out a little object that was about the size of a vitamin. He squeezed its sides, and it blinked to electronic life. It rose slowly into the air and hovered a few inches from his nose.

"Sentry, scan this immediate area, then take a position directly overhead, one hundred feet up."

The little drone did as instructed, and Zak walked back into the cave. Deragon had been busy setting up a sleeping spot for them. Marking out two spots roughly four feet wide and six feet long, he placed eight tiny objects that looked like coins at each corner then he tapped each one, and the ultron repulsers hummed to life. Then he placed eight more at the corners of where one would expect there to be pillows. These, somehow, seemed to be hovering in the air, when in reality they were laying on the unseen magnetic/energy cushions the first eight had caused.

Deragon looked over at Andromeda, gazing deeply into her green eyes one more time. He winked at her, both eyelids of his left eye snapping down and up smoothly. Then he laid down. It looked just as if he was laying in the air a foot off of the ground, flat on his back, head on the softest of pillows.

Zak followed suit, gazing with a confident smile into her blue eyes, the last sight he wanted to see before he went to sleep for the night, curled up on his side.

"What an amazing creature," Deragon thought to himself, and then fell fast asleep.

"What a woman," Zak thought to himself, and then he fell fast asleep.

"Fools!" Andromeda screamed inside her head, "could you not just go and do what I brought you here for?" And then she huffed in frustration before heading to her room in the back of the cave to retire for the night. It was certainly no use staying up; she had no influence over the minds of sleeping creatures.

CHAPTER ELEVEN

The day came early on Velaronas Four, but that did not bother Zak or Deragon. Professional mischief makers tended to sleep very lightly, if at all, since they were always expecting an angry knock on the door. The cave was a few thousand feet behind them as they descended into the valley, and Andromeda was still sleeping soundly within it. The sky this time of day was viridescent, and the same swirling breeze of yesterday was blowing again.

When Zak and Deragon began their trek, there was nothing to see in the valley below, as a haze was heavily resting upon it. The mountain peak across the valley, the point for which they were making, was easy to see, though.

"Our shortest path is obviously a straight line, but that haze in the valley worries me a bit. There is no telling what could be down there. What do you think?"

Deragon warbled and trilled, and from the tone alone Zak knew he was spoiling for a fight and ready for anything.

"Got it. Haze or no haze, we go straight. Get the job done, rescue the girl, be heroes, print t-shirts."

A tap of the energarmor, engage the weapons, and they were heading for the haze.

It took about an hour to reach the edge of the haze, and it had not lessened any by the time they arrived. It was odd, really, very much unlike anything they were familiar with on Earth or the Mars' colony. It seemed to be much like a vaporous blanket, but as they surveyed all directions around them, it was the only patch of haze or fog anywhere.

"Hafe gi wilo."

"Odd is a very good word for it."

Zak poked at the haze with the barrel of his weapon, and it parted to let the material in. When he withdrew it, it closed back up like a bucket of water would do if you stuck your finger in and then pulled it out. Taking a slow breath, Zak stepped down into it, and once more it parted ahead of him. Deragon followed, and in just a few steps they were completely enveloped.

Breathing was a bit strained, kind of like trying to breathe in a sauna. The haze, though, was truly remarkable. It continually opened ahead of them and shut behind them, and if they were not going steadily downhill, they would have very quickly been lost and disoriented.

"I really don't like this, not even a little."

Deragon responded with several rapid clicks that Zak knew meant that his friend was somewhere between annoyed and worried. When they had started out so early in the morning, it had been with enough overconfidence to take on an army by themselves. Somehow, the sight of a beautiful Tarq/girl would do that, I suppose. But the haze, while clouding their pathway, had cleared their minds. There was presently no thought of the beautiful Andromeda Tellecraft, there was just a realization by both that this was not what they had intended to get into when they escaped from Earth. This was supposed to be one permanent vacation, all fun and no responsibility, a chance to finally be themselves.

Instead, they had somehow been roped into being heroes, and heroes had a nasty tendency to get themselves killed.

Since they entered the haze, there had been nothing at all to hear other than the sound of their own breathing, their sporadic conversation, and their footsteps on the hard, rocky ground. Nothing to hear, almost nothing to see, an oppressive heaviness in the air, a growing agitation in both of them...

And then it all changed, in a blinding moment of time.

The second they stepped out of the haze, the light made them drop to their knees and snap their eyes shut. Tears were instantly streaming down their faces.

"It's like that the first time you come down out of the barrier."

They could not see the speaker, but the voice was clearly that of a little girl, maybe ten or twelve years old. She was speaking a different language than anyone they had ever met, including Andromeda. The beauty of the neuro-implanted universal translators that everyone on Earth or her colonies now had from birth was that whenever you heard a language you did not know, it would inform you that it was going to work, then immediately translate it for you, seamlessly, using the speaker's natural voice. It would also translate your words for the speaker using your natural voice. Once you did know a language, just like Zak knew Tarq, it would let your brain do the work. No matter where they went in the universe, Zak and Deragon would be able to understand anyone and anything speaking to them.

Within half a minute or so, both Zak and Deragon were able to begin blinking their eyes open, and they got back up onto their feet. Standing in front of them was, at least in appearance, a human little girl. She had pigtails and freckles, wide eyes, and a crooked smile.

"Where are we?"

"You are in The Valley."

Zak dared not make a sarcastic comment about the unbelievable obviousness of that answer. This was just a kid, and she may be of some help to them.

"Yes, thank you, I actually sort of figured that we were. Does this place have a name?"

"Yes. We call it The Valley."

64

Deragon actually snort-laughed at that. He was getting a kick out of seeing his buddy befuddled by a simple child.

Zak cut a glare back at Deragon, then turned back to face the child once more.

"The Valley. Ok, thanks. That is quite a nice name for it. And what is your name?"

"My name is Sybillia."

"Sybillia. That is a lovely name as well. Sybillia, what can you tell me about that?"

Zak was pointing past the girl to the amazing sight that lay beyond her. Going through The Valley may have provided the straightest path between the two peaks, but it might not at all be the quickest. For there, just below them, was a sprawling city.

CHAPTER TWELVE

Sybillia smiled that crooked smile again.

"That is a city," she said matter of factly.

This time, Deragon laughed right out loud. He liked this girl! Anyone who could frustrate Zak Blue like this had a lot of potential in his book.

"Yes, thank you," Zak smiled back, but the strain in his voice was clearly increasing. "Could you tell me what city it is, and who lives there?"

"Why certainly!" she said with unabashed joy. "That is Klingscleft. I live there, and so does Frezen Dergish, Solowat Jegins, Teppin Nomar, Waylo Ontax, Jellat Bokish, Fregar Buntea..."

"STOP! Stop, please, I'm sorry, let me rephrase that."

Deragon had lost it. He was literally laying on the ground, holding his sides laughing. Zak's head was spinning. He had no trouble talking to people who were complicated in their thinking. But a girl this simple in her thinking was absolutely killing him.

"I don't actually need you to tell me the name of every single person who lives there. Could you just tell me, in general, what race or nation or group of people you are? Specifically, are you the people of King Tellecraft?"

"I have never heard of a King Tellecraft," she said, "but I can tell you that we, the people who live here, are the Ryannis. Come, I will take you into the city. The elders will want to meet you."

"Finally," Zak mumbled to himself, "progress!"

Deragon picked himself up, dusted himself off, and followed, giggling most of the way.

The city, as I said, was sprawling. It was probably two or three miles long and wide and was apparently a city made of stone and clay. Yet the buildings themselves were not old looking, or haphazard. They were all three stories high or less, perfectly square, and the street structure was well organized. Simple people, simple layout.

Sybillia led the way, her steps never hesitating as she went. Within a matter of moments, they were all leaving the sandy slopes, and their feet were beginning to click on lovely cobblestones that would have seemed perfectly appropriate for nineteenth century London.

The people of the city would not have seemed out of place in the good old city either.

Their clothes were plain, their mannerisms curious but polite. Old men tipped their hats to them as they passed, little girls peeked at them shyly, and young boys just gawked. It was one of those gawking boys, rapidly consuming something that was by visual appearances akin to an apple, who first spoke.

"Hey, Syb, whatcha got there, a boyfriend and a pet?"

He laughed a deep belly laugh as he said it, but Deragon was not laughing.

"Easy, D," Zak said under his breath as he put his hand on his friend's forearm, mostly to keep him from doing something violent and rash, "let's not disintegrate anyone just yet."

"Hush up, Frezen," Sybillia said sharply, "and try not to make me mad today."

The boy went a bit white at that, and Zak raised his eyebrows in a bit of surprise. This girl must be a tough cookie!

She kept leading on, not even slacking her pace. They passed what appeared to be a fish market on the left, though the fish were not like any that either of them had ever seen. A pottery shop up ahead on the right, some type of a fruit stand a bit farther, all kinds of shops offering repairs on items that they had never heard of, random unlabeled buildings that appeared to be something like apartments, places to eat, places to enjoy entertainment: the city seemed to have it all, in an old-yet-interesting sort of way.

Rounding a corner to the left, the buildings seemed to get bigger and nicer, and the street wider. There were statues of portly, smiling people and odd-shaped monuments seemingly made of material far too nice for the setting.

"Government row, D, mark my words. Wherever there is a row of portly, polished pointy-heads on nice wide streets, that is where people have chosen to perpetually pat themselves on the back while telling others how low they are."

Deragon warbled and shook his head a bit. Zak always did have trouble with authority, and his encounter with Tiller Mansen seemed to have sent him even more deeply into that abyss.

Ten minutes more of brisk walking and they found themselves climbing a slightly curved stone staircase up toward a lovely, low-slung building. It had a pinkish hue that seemed to stick out like a sore thumb and more of the statues which were making Zak more of a sore fugitive.

Reaching the top of the stairs, Sybillia continued right along toward the large triple doors. Without so much as a knock, she barged right in, and Zak instinctively reached out and grabbed her gently by the arm.

"Hey, um, shouldn't you knock, or call, or make an appointment or something?"

Sybillia raised one eyebrow, cocked her head in bewilderment, and said, "Why, whatever for? This is where our government meets! Come on, let's go speak to the elders."

CHAPTER THIRTEEN

The flesh and blood versions of the polished pointy-heads they had passed on their way in seemed every bit as stuffy as Zak had expected them to be. Still, as he sat across the old fashioned, yet incredibly beautiful, wooden table from them, he had to admit they were, in many regards, far different from what one could expect back on Earth. Never would Earth politicos tolerate any of the "unwashed masses" barging in and simply having a seat at the table.

Sybillia sat to his right, chattering away, while the men simply stared at her and nodded politely. Deragon was to his left and was not being looked at any differently than anyone else, though Zak doubted of any of these people had ever seen anyone quite like him before.

As Zak mused on all of this, his thoughts were suddenly snapped back to attention by a surprisingly deep voice, so deep as to seem almost bear-like.

"So, Mr. Blue, of a world called 'Earth,' is it? Please accept the warmest of welcomes from myself and all of the elders of Klingscleft. I am glad Sybillia has brought you to us. We so very rarely have visitors anymore,"

"Since the barrier was put in place," interjected a wizened old man off to the left of the original speaker.

"Yes, since the barrier was put in place."

Zak seemed to sense a bit of irritation from "Mr. Bear Voice" as he repeated what "Mr. Wizzy" had said. Apparently the barrier was not something to be freely discussed. Zak knew he would have to tread carefully if he expected to learn anything. But, thankfully, "important people" everywhere can be counted on in at least one regard; they will be proud to a fault. *Play on that pride, Zak*, he thought to himself, *and the keys to the kingdom are yours, so to speak.*

"The barrier," he whistled as his eyes grew wide in seeming amazement. "That is a marvel if I have ever seen one! Yes, sir, it must have taken some incredibly brilliant men, top of the line intellects, to produce such a wonder. Tell me, how did you men do it, and what is its purpose?"

Every face at the table flushed red with a mixture of pomposity and embarrassment. None of these men had anything to do with the creation of that fiendish fog, Zak knew that. They were mere children compared to whoever created it. But he also knew that none of them would ever admit it, especially in front of little Sybillia, the trusting and talkative citizen looking up at them in rapturous expectation of what they would say. That being the case, they would hem and haw over its creation and creators, and then to make up for that, would spill their guts as to its purpose.

Three, two, one... he counted to himself in his head...

"Um, yes, the barrier, a marvel it is indeed, an absolute marvel. Took a great deal of thought and study to produce that, advanced mathematics, specialized science, things like that, things we would never dream of boring you with.

"It was, er, we put it in place a great many years ago. It lets in the light for us each day, but blocks out, um, hinders, ah..."

"It keeps the madness from coming!"

Mr. Wizzy to the rescue, Zak inwardly grinned to himself. But that inward grin left almost as quickly as it came. Everyone at that table, even Mr. Bear Voice, was clearly frightened.

"Lucian, calm yourself. There is no need to trouble our guest about such things."

Zak knew he needed to push; he could not let this opportunity slip away.

"I am not troubled in the least, sir. In fact, my companion and I are intrigued. Our world is so very far away; we are explorers, of sorts. And we would love to know what madness this is of which you speak and how the barrier prevents it. It may be that perhaps we could even be of some assistance."

"We need no assistance," snapped a thin, sullen, sunken-eyed man at the end of the table. "The barrier keeps the madness from coming, that is all."

"It most certainly is not all," Sybillia said sweetly and matter of factly. Amazingly, the clearly powerful men seated around the table simply bowed to her just a bit and let her continue.

"There has been no madness in my lifetime, as the barrier has always been in place. But my mother has told me many stories of what it was like before the barrier came. The Valley had always been such a peaceful place, but then the peace stopped. People began to argue, and scream, and even hurt each other."

Sybillia had started the ball rolling, and now everyone at the table seemed to feel free to chime in one after the other.

"I remember it. My best friend and I were very little. We were eating our afternoon meal when he suddenly snatched a stibble fruit out of my basket. He knew that it was my last one and that it was my favorite!"

Apparently "Mr. Stibble" was not the only one at the table there on that day of his great offense.

"I most certainly did not, and I will thank you not to start telling that old lie of a yarn all over again! You held it out to me with your own hand and gave it to me, a 'symbol of our everlasting friendship,' you called it. Then as soon as I bit into it, you acted as if I had snatched it from you by force!"

"Small rofendas," snapped a very dark man across the table. "My own parents appeared and disappeared before my very eyes! Mother would call me into the back yard to feed the persiputs, and then as soon as I got out there she would be gone, then a moment later be screaming at me from the upper floors of our house, demanding that I obey her at once and fold my clothes. No sooner would I start running that way than she and my father both would be found sitting around the table, staring at me in bewilderment as I tried to explain my rushing about. I was sent for counseling my entire young life, and to this day have blemishes on my psychological record.

"Piddldywinks," guffawed Mr. Bear Voice. "My own father left home and never returned, he said it was haunted. I raised myself in that place and have to admit that he was right. Things and people would appear and then disappear. I would be putting a sandwich to my mouth and take a bite into nothing but air. The most blessed of our days in Klingscleft was when the barrier was put in place. True, it has restricted our movements, but The Valley provides us all that we need, and no one has experienced the madness since the day we awoke to find the barrier above us."

Now that last part Zak did not want to hear. Mr. Bear Voice had just unwittingly admitted to something that would be a stumbling block on this quest; not only did none of these men make the barrier, none of them had so much as a clue where it came from or how it worked.

The conversation turned to more mundane issues after that, the men around the table seemed intent on it doing so. Fear is like that; once you have spilled your guts on it, the embarrassment makes you clam up pretty quickly, and these men were afraid. They had their barrier, the madness could not get to them, and they were content.

In the middle of a veritable prison, they were content.

CHAPTER FOURTEEN

Sybillia was gone, the doors of the town hall were closed behind them, and Zak and Deragon sat on the steps munching on the fruit the town elders had so hospitably loaded them down with on their way out.

"Stibble fruit," Zak said as a bit of the juice trickled down his hands, "I can't really see why there would be a fight over it. Tastes a lot like a vegobar, honestly."

He spat out the bite and took a sip of water.

"So what do we have here, D?"

Deragon let out a low, long whistle, as he shook his head slowly. Then he trilled and warbled for a few minutes, all of which Zak understood perfectly.

"Yes, it would seem so. Nothing that Andromeda said matches anything that we have yet seen. It may be that she herself is a victim of the madness. For her own safety, as much as I

77

despise the thought of anyone being trapped, we may have to get her into the valley."

"Lina torva da sorceressi?"

"Well, I think it is pretty clear that the sorceress is the source of the madness, and as such, if we can deal with her, we may solve everyone's problems at once."

Deragon cocked his head sideways as he watched his buddy take the next sip. This was a bit disconcerting, honestly. To hear Zak speaking in selfish terms would not so much have registered with him. To hear him speak of "solving everyone's problems at once," that was odd, very odd.

"Shadai ewet engor Da Valcona Celesto?"

"No. Until we know what we are dealing with, I will not put the Falcon Wing at risk. She is our ticket to the universe, buddy, and the only thing able to outrun our pursuers. We go on foot, we deal with the threat, and then we figure out where to go from there."

A few minutes later there was a stibble core laying on the steps, courtesy of a young man whose manners were still suspect at best. Zak and Deragon were on their way toward the far edge of town, and a healthy crowd of gawkers grew in number the nearer they came to the far edge of the barrier.

And then they were gone, disappearing into the fog, leaving the people of Klingscleft to go about their daily lives.

"This is something else, D," Zak grunted. "Whoever put this barrier in place was not some run of the mill dummy."

Deragon whistled behind him. Their eyes were adjusting yet again, and they once more trusted to the slope of the ground as they chose their course, this time upward instead of downward. As they were more familiar with the fog, it did not take them quite as long to get out as it did to get in, but once again, when they burst out of it into the daylight, they sunk to their knees as their eyes rebelled against the brightness of the light. Finally, they were able to stand, to blink, and to see.

"I am a genius, D, and even I can't figure out how such an impenetrable fog allows light down into the valley while simultaneously keeping out whatever cause the madness. But it is likely that we will find our answers up ahead, somewhere in or on that mountain peak.

Without a word, they set off on a near run. They would have liked nothing better than to go and finish the job, but their time in Klingscleft had cost them dearly. After an hour of hard hoofing it, covering maybe three miles, the day was already waning fast, and they would not make it to the mountain before nightfall.

"Ewet gopha gian ut hacer compa."

"I agree. May as well get started then. You set up shelter, I will do a quick scouting of the area."

Deragon went to work, locating a nice cove under an outcropping of rock. True, they

79

could have simply fabricated an energon tent, but somehow real shelter, even rudimentary real shelter, always felt more homey.

Zak pulled a few more sentry drones out of his tool belt, squeezed their sides, and they began to hover in front of him, awaiting his instructions.

"We are taking no chances. All of you go to two hundred feet and maintain a constant rotating perimeter of one mile around us. If anything bigger than a gopher breaches that perimeter, I want to know about it immediately. In fact, do a full rotation and scan of the area right now and tell me what you see."

The drones shot away from him like bees amped up on an energy drink. They did their mission fast, just fifteen minutes, but very thoroughly. When they sent a signal that they had all of the data, Zak barked two simple words: "Project, transmit."

From a link button on his chest, a hologram popped into view standing just a few feet in front of him. It was a hologram of himself. It was only natural he would program his drones to project that image, I suppose, given his inherent arrogance.

"Zak, my man!" the hologram began, "You are looking as good as ever!"

Zak smiled a bit of an ironic smile as his eyes fell on the one visual difference between the two of them. The hologram did not have his new white streak running down the side of his blonde head of hair.

I'll have to update that, I suppose, Zak thought to himself, and then he responded to the image in front of him, "You as well, Zak Bluetoo! What do you have for me?"

"I have clear skies, peaceful surroundings, nothing with so much as a big enough fang or sharp enough claw to cause you any issues. But just to make sure you get plenty of good beauty sleep, me and my boys will do an all-night hover round. If anything ooly comes around, we will gently scream into your ear, and then sit back and watch the fun."

"Good enough," Zak said, and then with a wave of his hand, his digital alter ego disappeared.

"What about it D, are we set up for the night?"

A satisfied trill and whistle and Zak knew everything would be fine. He turned and made for the shelter, as he mumbled to himself, "Tomorrow, Sorceress, tomorrow we will find out what you are made of."

CHAPTER FIFTEEN

The smell of bacon frying in the morning is one that has transcended the ages. Those scofflaws from Earth, who had rebelled against government mandated blandness in food, would trade in lengths of bacon like some kind of ancient bootleggers, often fetching an exorbitant sum for their efforts. Naturally, Zak had not objected to that trade, in fact, he had been at various times both a salesman and a customer.

But this, this heavenly, powerful, abundant smell, this was just beyond description! As his eyes opened, he inhaled very deeply, until it felt like his lungs would explode. His head sunk into the soft downy pillow in sheer ecstasy, the covers seem to hug him like a mother's love...

And instantly he was rolling up onto one knee with his weapon pointed ahead of him, every sense hyper-alert, his finger already half-way depressing the trigger.

Laughter. Soft, billowy, grandmotherly type laughter.

"Calm down, dearie, there is no need to be tense and frightened. Come, come, join your friend at the table."

The cottage was warm and cozy. There was a fire in the fireplace on which the bacon was cooking. Two windows, one on each side of the room. Only one door, meaning only one way of escape if needed, and a way that could easily be blocked. No matter, he would blow the roof off of this place if needed.

There was a table in the middle of the room, and Deragon was already at it, looking to be about half way done with breakfast. He waved at Zak cheerfully, then went back to his eating as if he had never tasted anything so amazing.

The bed Zak had just rolled out of was at the back of the room. One a few feet away from it was mussed up, with a blanket void that was about the size of Deragon.

"Where am I, and how did I get here, speak now if you want to live."

More billowy laughter as the old woman continued to bustle about the kitchen.

"You don't want to shoot me, or anyone else for that matter. The morning is too nice, the food too fresh, the day too filled with promise. Come, dear one, come and sit and eat. You are in my cottage, and in my cottage there is peace."

Zak tentatively sheathed his weapon, rose to his feet and made his way to the table. Every sense was still on high alert, not because the present surrounding seemed dangerous, it surely seemed anything but, in fact, but because he could not remember how he had gotten here. The last thing he remembered was navigating the Leonid Expulsion, and he felt like he vaguely recalled passing out and sliding onto the floor.

If you are a Tarq, the smell of dolphus eggs frying in the morning is one that you never forget. Deragon had loved that smell as a child and loved it still. It was deep and pungent. Humans seemed to intently dislike it, but then, their taste simply could not be accounted for. They would eat strips of pig, fried to a crisp, for goodness sake. No wonder their taste buds were so malformed!

But this, this heavenly, powerful, abundant smell, this was just beyond description! As his eyes opened, he inhaled very deeply, until it felt like his lungs would explode. His head sunk into the soft downy pillow in sheer ecstasy, the covers seem to hug him like a mother's love...

And instantly he was rolling up onto one knee, two small yet deadly hand pulsars pointed ahead of him, every sense hyper-alert, his wrists halfway clenched into firing position.

Laughter. Soft, billowy, grandmotherly type laughter.

"Xaler peri, sucra, blee gana ona tejar ut ba hypru kai phobre. Aqu, aqu, lunkar oya dana ta da mesor."

The cottage was warm and cozy. There was a fire in the fireplace on which the dolphus eggs were cooking. Two windows, one on each side of the room. Only one door, meaning only one way of escape if needed, and a way that could easily be blocked. No matter, he would die right here fighting for his friend if needed.

There was a table in the middle of the room, and Zak was already at it, looking to be about half way done with breakfast. He waved at Deragon cheerfully, then went back to his eating as if he had never tasted anything so amazing.

The bed Deragon had just rolled out of was at the back of the room. One a few feet away from it was completely unmade, typical of Zak.

"Ajij eimi O?"

More billowy laughter as the old woman continued to bustle about the kitchen.

"Oyt eimi en mou casoma."

Deragon tentatively retracted his weapons, rose to his feet, and made his way to the table. Every sense was still on high alert. Not because the present surrounding seemed dangerous, it surely seemed anything but, in fact, but because he could not remember how he had gotten here. The last thing he remembered was holding on for dear life as Zak navigated the Leonid Expulsion.

Many miles away, Andromeda was fuming. Her carefully laid plans were going awry, partially because of the unpredictable impetuosity of Zak Blue and partially because of the growing power of her sister Castella. Sorceress? Certainly not, neither of them were. Their kind were very ancient, very powerful, very misunderstood, and nearly always unappreciated. But their power, erratic, dangerous, and maddening, was purely mental. Not a one of their kind possessed much at all in the way of physical strength. Their generations had positively withered physically from the strong creatures they once were as they spent century after century delving deeper and deeper into the recesses of the power of the mind.

Castella was ruining everything and had to be destroyed. Zak Blue was her means to that end. But he and his reptile friend were, for the moment, under the spell of Castella's mind. Andromeda could see them sitting dumbfounded under the cleft of the rock they had slept under, staring straight ahead, drooling and mumbling.

The drones had not been so much as an ounce of help, for no one, not even Castella, had come near them. They had gone to sleep close enough to her sphere of influence that she did not need to. From her perch on the mountainside, she waved her hands gently, whispered to the wind, and was now manipulating their minds like mere marionettes.

"So how did you come to this place, grandmother?"

"Oh dearie," the old woman mused, "I have been here for a hundred years or more, I suppose, and my family for far longer than that."

As she poured each of them a refill of their drinks, both Zak and Deragon could not help but feel a bit of a tug at their hearts, for to each of them, she looked surprisingly like their own grandmothers. Why they had been so tense was simply beyond them. However they had gotten here, it really did not matter, they were in a wonderful place.

"We certainly appreciate your hospitality. I am sorry we cannot tell you more of how we came here, but it seems that neither of us remembers. The quaver rays must have affected us in ways that we cannot yet understand. I just hope everything comes back to us soon. It is hard to get where you are going when you don't even know how you got to where you are, or where you were headed before you arrived!"

The grandmother smiled sweetly. "Take your time, dearies, once you get back to the Falcon Wing, everything will come back to you." And then she breathed a sigh, a heavy-hearted, weight-of-the-world kind of sound, and shook her head as she mumbled softly, "and when it does, just think of me kindly. I am not long at all for this world, now that she has come."

CHAPTER SIXTEEN

"What do you mean, grandmother? Who has come, and how is she bothering you?"

Both Zak and Deragon had, even without realizing it, become fiercely protective of this sweet old lady. Somewhere along the line, it occurred to them both that she was, in fact, his grandmother. Zak had loved this woman who had taken him in when his own parents cast him out. Deragon had fond memories of her rocking him to sleep with a Verusian lullaby. She had clothed them, fed them...

"I am the dearest person in the universe to you," Castella whispered into their minds, "you cannot let anyone hurt me..."

"Ewet gopha mayginoin permis tis ut anath oyt."

"I know you won't, dearie, I know you won't. Now, listen to me very carefully, both of you. Go back immediately to your ship. Do not under any circumstances go back into the valley.

It will take you much longer, but you must go around it. Go to the Falcon Wing and destroy Andromeda at once! If you do not, she will kill me, she will kill your sweet grandmother. Go! Go, hurry! There is not a moment to lose!"

Andromeda watched from her side of the valley and Castella watched from hers as Zak and Deragon jumped up and bolted off like they had been shot out of a cannon. Now it would be a battle of their two minds; Castella would exert all of her power to keep them under her spell long enough to destroy Andromeda, and Andromeda would try mightily to wrestle them back under her power to destroy her sister Castella.

"Who will it be, Castella, the temptress or the grandmother, the seductress or the nostalgic? Which one of us will win?"

Castella thought her response back as clearly as if she had been standing beside her to speak, "I am sure you think it will be the seductress. Your mind has always gone to the obvious yet erroneous. The nostalgic has been with them for far longer, though, and there is no way you will break my control over them. Prepare to meet your end, sister," Castella said with a fiendish laugh of triumph.

"Actually, my overconfident sister, you might want to rethink your plan. In fact, we both might."

Castella returned her attention to Zak and Deragon and gasped at the same time as Andromeda.

Zak and Deragon were at that very second plunging headlong into the barrier.

While Andromeda and Castella had been somewhat preoccupied with each other, Zak and Deragon had been gasping and talking in strained snatches as they ran.

"Lina gi da skema?"

"Pretty simple. We take the shortest route possible back to the Falcon Wing, blow Andromeda out of the water, and make sure no one ever hurts grandmother again."

Deragon huffed and puffed both through his mouth and his gills as he tried to keep up.

"Pero eva rhema ut sajay cerco da blockut."

"Yeah, D, I know she told us to go around the barrier. But c'mon, it is the straightest way. She's probably just worried about us. For her sake, we have to do it our way."

As that last word came out of his mouth, Zak and Deragon plunged headlong into the fog. As before, it parted just ahead of them, and continually closed up behind them.

"Hafe gi meno wilo."

"Yep, still odd. But at least we know what we are dealing with this time."

The trip back down into the valley took about the same amount of time as before, right about an hour or so. And, though they continually reminded themselves to be ready for it, once again the plunging out of the fog into the brightness of the light caught them off guard.

"Ow, just ow."

Like Zak, Deragon was also on his knees, shaking his head, blinking.

"It's like that the second time you come down out of the barrier, too."

Now Deragon was no longer on his knees. The sound of Sybillia's familiar voice, the obvious prospect of a round two of Zak Blue frustration, the fact that she was somehow, inexplicably right there when they came out of the fog again, it was simply too much for him. He was now laying on his side, curled up in a fetal position shaking with convulsive laughter.

"Zip it, fish face," Zak said in exasperation. But Deragon did not zip it, Zak's comment just made him laugh that much harder.

"You came back," Sybillia said simply.

"Yes, we did, thank you for telling us that," Zak said curtly.

"If you were going to come back, wouldn't it have been quicker just to stay?"

Now Deragon was laughing so hard that he could not catch his breath!

"Yes, Sybillia, yes, it would have been. But if we had stayed, we would not have left. And if we would not have left, we would not have found my grandmother, so I would say our departure was beneficial."

Despite his convulsive laughter, Deragon caught Zak's usage of the personal pronoun "my." He was about to correct Zak when Sybillia spoke again.

"If your world is so far away, how did your grandmother get here?"

Laughter? No. None. If jaws dropping make a sound, then the sound of Deragon and Zak's jaws dropping would have been deafening. After what could only make a pregnant pause seem short by comparison, Zak spoke, lowly, slowly, carefully.

"Buddy, I think we have been, to quote old-timey Earth movies, 'royally played.'"

Deragon just whistled in stunned agreement. He did not know what to do or think and, worse than that, it was pretty clear his genius buddy who always had all the answers (albeit usually answers that consistently got them into trouble) did not know what to think either. It was Sybillia, utterly simple minded Sybillia who gave genius and sidekick the answer that should have been obvious.

"It is the madness. Anytime one is outside of the barrier, he is at risk. In here we are safe. You should stay here forever."

Zak grinned a weak yet grateful grin. "Sweet Sybillia, I appreciate that, I really do. But what in the world is there here for a couple of rogues like us? Being stibble fruit farmers would not exactly suit us, I think."

"No, maybe not," she said with a cock of her head. What she said next, simply read on a page, would sound insulting. But trust me when I tell you that as she said it, it came across with

93

such utter innocence, neither Zak nor Deragon was insulted in the least. In fact, they were both instantly, thoroughly intrigued:

"People like you would probably be trouble makers here, wanting to go through the old records, trying to find out about the madness and the barrier, and making the elders get nervous. It would probably make everyone happier if you leave. Except for you, of course, since you will have your minds taken again when you do. Oh well, goodbye!"

She turned and started to skip back down toward the town.

She made it about two skips before Zak had her gently yet firmly by one arm and Deragon by the other.

"Whoa, whoa, hold up just a minute, Syb. Did you say 'records'? Records concerning the madness and the barrier?"

"I sure did," she smiled sweetly, "in fact, I said, 'People like you would probably be trouble makers here, wanting to go through the old records, trying to find out about the madness and the barrier, and making the elders get nervous. It would probably make everyone happier if you leave. Except for you, of course, since you will have your minds taken again when you do. Oh well, goodbye!' "

"Yes, you did, yes, you did. Sybillia, I need to know about those records. Where would I find them?"

"Silly, you would find them where you find everything else, you would find them where they are at!"

"Yes, of course, I would. And, if I wanted to go where they are at so that I could find them, where would I be going to be there?"

Zak knew that question was incredibly disjointed, but he was trying to pick up on the learning curve when it came to communication with this girl. He found out quickly that he was onto something.

"Why," she smiled that crooked grin, "you would be going to the hall of records, where the records are kept. Of course, it really isn't a hall at all, more like a really large room."

"Right, hall of records, a really large room. If your world is anything like mine, that would probably be right in the government district, correct?"

"Yes," she said solemnly. "But no one can go in there, even though they can."

Now that one stumped him.

"What do you mean?"

"We have been told to stay out, so no one can go in there, even though they can since the door is always unlocked."

"Seriously? There is a forbidden room, unlocked, and no one goes in there? Why?"

"Because we have been told not to."

"Right, right."

Zak looked over at Deragon, whose eyes were wide with amazement. Could it really be this easy? He had been expecting another "make a break for it and then run for your life" moment.

"Sybillia, we do not want to get you into trouble, but I need to, um, I am curious as to where that room is."

"Whatever for? You cannot go in it."

"Yes, I know. But um..."

And then the stroke of genius hit him:

"But I need to know where it is so that I can be sure to not go in it! If I do not know where it is, I may accidentally find it and wander into it. If I know where it is, I can avoid it!"

Zak smiled a fake million-dollar smile. Sybillia smiled a genuine, worth-more-than-all-of-the-money-in-the-world smile. Deragon grimaced to himself. His buddy was lying. Again. For a good cause? Maybe, but still...

"I understand!" Sybillia said with glee. "Come with me, and I will show you where not to go!"

And then she was off like a flash, skipping down the hillside. Zak and Deragon followed hard after her. The kid was fast!

The trip was a near perfect opposite of the one they had taken while on the way out of town. Back past the same houses on the outskirts, the same shops and markets further in, a turn down government avenue, and then right back up the steps of city hall. Once more bursting in the doors, and then, this time a change, a quick dip down a flight of stairs to the right, winding, winding, winding, winding...

"Ewet eimi uhna mihlor hodos peri!"

"Yes, we are going a long way down," Zak whispered in a puff of breath. "Whoever put these down here did not want them to be much thought of or sought out."

Fifteen stories beneath the surface, the stairs ended. And there, ten feet ahead of them, was a massive set of old wooden double doors, and on those doors a sign, "Keep Out!"

CHAPTER SEVENTEEN

"You see?" Sybillia said with the utmost of seriousness, "No one can go in." And then the seriousness was immediately gone, the smile was back, and she chirped "But now that you know where you cannot go, you know where you can go! One only has to know the one to know the other, you know."

Now that, Zak had to admit, was truly intelligent. He had no intention of going along with it, but it was intelligent nonetheless.

"You are exactly right, Sybillia. And now that we know where we cannot go, we better go ahead and leave. We would not want your parents to be worried about you, now would we?"

The three made their way back up the steps, and all of them would have told you that steps are much easier going down than up. Except for maybe Sybillia, who chirped cheerfully the entire way back up, prattling on about everything and nothing. By the time fifteen flights of steps had been put behind them, Zak was truly ready to part from his gullible guide for a while.

"Thank you, Sybillia, thank you. Now, I have one more question for you before we part ways. If Deragon and I wanted to be alone for a while to rest, where would you recommend that we go?"

Somehow, as soon as he said it, he knew, he just knew he shouldn't have.

"Why, if you want to be alone, I would suggest you go where no one else is already at! Goodbye!" And then she skipped away, leaving Deragon on the floor in one last fit of laughter.

Miles away, Andromeda paced in her cave in frustration. It had been bad enough that her private playground, otherwise known as "banishment," had to be shared with her sister. Now she was having to deal with the irritation of two utter fools who could have given her everything she needed and yet were doing everything wrong.

Miles away on the other side of the valley, Castella was matching her pacing step for step and her musing thought for thought.

The light coming through the barrier was fading. Zak and Deragon were sitting beside two trees maybe a half mile out of town and out of sight of any prying eyes.

"Rosem O balans tejar ut quilow, 'lina gi oya skema?'"

"No, you don't even need to ask. You know what the plan is without needing to ask, don't you, D?"

He did, in fact. They would wait until after dark, sneak back into town, go into the hall of records, and see if they could find something to help them with their task. But even as that thought rumbled around in his partially reptilian head, Deragon could not help but to be amazed at it. Why were they even still here?

Fact number one, this place and this situation was clearly a danger to them.

Fact number two, Zak Blue could call for the Falcon Wing, she would come right to them inside the barrier, and within seconds, they could be on their way away from this place heading for some more safe and sane world.

Fact number three, he knew that if he had already thought of those first two facts, then Zak had as well. And that confused him mightily. Zak had to know by now, as he did, that since their minds were being messed with, there was neither a sultry seductress on one side of them nor a sweet grandmother on the other. There was nothing here for them but trouble, and yet they were still here. What was happening to the Zak Blue he had come to accept through the years, the self-centered, arrogant, egotistical, rebellious, dishonest, and impetuous friend that really was a friend to him despite all of those negative traits?

True, Zak had lied just a couple of hours earlier, and to an innocent little girl at that. But even that thought perplexed him because there was no profit to it. In fact, there was nothing good for them that could come from staying here another minute, let alone wading into huge potential trouble. The fact that the doors were unlocked meant nothing. They were unlocked simply because no one had ever been complicated enough to go in. Let someone go in, and the kind elders of the city would cease to be kind in the blink of an eye. Deragon was certain of this, and he was certain that Zak was certain of it. So what was going on?

"Our answers are down there in that room, D, all of them! The barrier, the two mind twisting whatever they ares, all of our answers are down there. Before this night is done, we will have them. I...will...know."

Suddenly it clicked with Deragon. His mind played it back for him like an ancient recorder: "He said 'again,' D."

Was that what this was about? Did Tiller Mansen's taunt really get under Zak Blue's skin so badly? Was this going to change him from a carefree bird in the wind to some crusader? Or was Deragon simply overreacting, overthinking?

"Let's go," Zak said as the last ray of light faded from view. With a wave of the hand in front of their faces, the energon generated night vision visor came online for them both. Away from the tree they went, down the hill stealthily, heading for goodness knows what kind of modern day boy scout, goody-two-shoes adventure Zak was leading them into.

CHAPTER EIGHTEEN

To say that the town of Klingscleft was quite at night would be an understatement. The ancients used to say of quiet country towns "they roll the sidewalks up at sundown." Here it was more like they rolled the sidewalks up, cut the power, played a universal lullaby, and both sides of the pillow were cool.

Nonetheless, Zak and Deragon moved as furtively as if they were being tracked by snifferbots. *Take no chances, Zak, take no chances*, he kept whispering inside his head. Funny, that; why should he be whispering inside his head? After all, no one could hear it. So, just to break the norm, just to feed his rebellious nature, he shouted it inside his head, then screamed it, then screamed it while beating a huge drum.

Take that, pointy-headed politicians of every planet and system, he whispered to himself inside his head yet again.

The trip back up into city hall took a good while, from post to post, hiding place to hiding place. But once they were inside, the trip down the fifteen flights of stairs flew by, and I mean literally. Count on Zak Blue to ride the banister of a fifteen flight set of spiral stairs! Naturally Deragon was right behind him. Zak came shooting off the end at the bottom, slid across the floor, and literally busted through the huge doors, with Deragon right on his heels.

Massive.

The place was utterly massive.

This place was not the Balindrome, but it surely felt like it. Towering ceilings, with bookshelves running from the floor to the ceilings, and each shelf packed with volumes. Millions...upon millions...of volumes. It would take a thousand lifetimes to even sneak a quick peak at the title on the spine of each one.

"They really don't have much of a need to put a lock on the doors, D, how could anybody ever find anything in here? It's a good thing we aren't just anybody, I suppose. Let's see if we can't speed up this process a bit. First, some help.

Once again Zak reached into his tool belt and pulled out a tiny mini drone, squeezed its sides, and it blinked and beeped to life.

As it hovered in front of him at eye level, Zak started giving it parameters.

"We are looking for one book or set of records in particular. These people will have 'hidden' it somewhere in here. But, they are very simple, so they will not have hidden it well.

Drone, begin by doing a complete scan, and find me the pattern of how they have all of this filed."

The drone was off at once. Half an hour later it was back hovering in front of him. A touch of the link button on his chest and Zak Bluetoo popped into view standing just a few feet in front of him once again.

"Hello there, my looting librarian, I have some good news and some bad news. The bad news is, there is absolutely no pattern to how any of this is filed. The good news is, I just saved fifteen percent on my car insurance!"

"Really?" Zak said to his digital alter ego with some annoyance, "a bad joke from some ancient commercial? That is the best you can do?"

"Sorry, real me, I just thought you might need some sugar to help the medicine go down. Seriously, though, this place is a mess, there is not an ounce of rhyme or reason to it."

Zak twisted his face to the side and pondered on that. In a way, it sort of fit. These were the simplest people he had ever met, so it sort of stood to reason that they would not use anything so complex as a rational filing system. Further, if there was something they did not want someone to read, they would not be suspicious enough to hide it well. In fact, they might not be suspicious enough to hide it at all. But they were clearly nervous over the whole barrier/madness thing, and even a bit embarrassed, so they would do something, but what?

"Whatever it is, D, it would seem incredibly devious to them. But their devious is so far beneath our devious that to us it would seem utterly childlike."

And then a thought hit him. Could it be that simple?

"Drone, while you were scanning, was there a volume that was turned pages out instead of spine out?"

"Yeah, man, one and only one. Looks like somebody got a little careless and no one ever fixed it."

"Wrong answer, Zak Bluetoo, somebody got incredibly, terribly, government conspiracy level sneaky! Why, this would make that Nixon guy from the twentieth century blush. Show me that book, right now!"

And with a flash the drone was off with Zak and Deragon in pursuit. Fifty yards down the center aisle, turn to the right down another, four hundred yards down that aisle, zig zag through a section of smaller shelves, and ten minutes later they were looking, (eye level, of course) at one book turned around backwards.

With trembling hands Zak pulled it out, turned it to where he could see the front cover, and read the title:

The Barrier, the Coming of the Mind Benders, and the Madness

By

Willifer Snodboddom

CHAPTER NINETEEN

"This book is huge, D, and not digital. Have a seat, I am going to speed read it, but even that will take a bit."

Deragon sat down by a bookshelf and cleaned the scales on the back of his hands. The hologram of Zak told one too many corny jokes, meaning "one," and Zak cut him off. He needed to concentrate.

After an hour, Zak whistled for Deragon.

"Check this out. The first half of the book was nothing but a description of how crazy everyone got, and man, did they get really far out there. And there is a trend to it. It started extremely small and for a long time stayed like that. But then it suddenly spiked, moving from little pranks to things that were outright deadly. People lost their lives, D, they killed each other in some maniacal madness.

"It was at that point that this Snodboddom guy, bless his adventurous little heart, started

111

doing some investigative work. He looked at the timing of the first reports of the madness, and then at the news reports, and I mean even tiny little trivial things did not escape his notice. Then he looked at the timing of the escalation in the madness and looked at all of the news reports again. He was smart enough to look for a common denominator, and he found it. Right before both, someone reported a falling star.

"Ol' Snoddy took the information straight to the elders of the town and, simpletons that they are, they blew him off. No falling star had ever caused them trouble before, so they extrapolated from that, that none ever would. Then they went back to trying to make better vitamins and ointments in the hope of curing the madness.

"Thank goodness Snoddy didn't give up. I think I would like this guy. Check this entry out."

Deragon took the book and read beginning at where Zak's finger was pointing.

Today is Alivia 43781, three contrauaks after the madness began. I have gotten nowhere with the elders, yet I am as convinced of my findings as ever. There is no other commonality, none. The falling stars coincide perfectly with the first events and with the obvious escalation. One began the madness, the other increased it to harmful, even deadly levels.

Do I believe that falling stars are to blame? No. But though our world chose many years ago to eschew the stars and any travel into them, the old writings are clear that beings have, for a very long time, traveled between worlds. Something came to our world on those falling rocks, if they were even rocks. More likely they were crafts of some kind.

One thing is clear, we are not alone. And if no one else will find out the who and the why of the madness, I will. Further, I will find a way to make it stop, or at least to defend against it. There is nothing the mind cannot achieve if it can think big enough yet plan minutely enough.

Tomorrow I will explore, tomorrow.

Deragon warbled and whistled, slowly and deliberately.

"Yeah, I agree. We are walking in dangerous footsteps, but the fact that someone left those footsteps gives us a fighting chance. This guy was something special. Without anywhere near our level of technology, he accomplished something far beyond his time. Having found the source, or sources, rather, of the problem, he made a way to defend against it. Check out this entry."

Deragon began to read again.

Hopeless, yes, hopeless. At least, hopeless in the sense of actually defeating these creatures. I do not know what to call them, I do not know what world they are from, but their powers of the mind are staggering. They can make us see what is not actually there, hear what no one has said, feel stimuli that do not exist, taste food that is purely imaginary, and smell odors where none truly are.

Worse still, they seem to thrive on producing conflict. I have watched family members literally come to blows, and worse. And somehow, the chaos they produce seems to make them stronger still. It is as if it is fuel for their growth just as food is fuel for ours.

And yet, their hatred for us seems to pale in comparison to their hatred for each other. Odd, that creatures so similar to each other and so different from us would not feel a kinship and kindness for each other.

The fights they are producing bear a commonality and tell me something of their personality. No material is ever carried out of the city, though they could easily compel people's minds and make them do so. Thus, their motives are entirely centered on the chaos itself, not on anything that can be gained from it.

That is utterly frightening; chaos for chaos sake can neither be reasoned with nor purchased away.

People at random times will rush out of the city toward the mountains on the west, hatred and murder in their eyes, then just as quickly rush back, bewildered. At other times, they will rush out of the city toward the mountains on the east, hatred and murder in their eyes, then just as quickly rush back, bewildered yet again.

I sense that neither is strong enough to overcome the other, both love to torment us, and neither will stop until we are their personal objects of twisted pleasure.

No, I cannot defeat them. But I can...I will...stop them.

"He did it, D, he built the barrier. Four chapters after this entry, he describes how he ended up in one of those brainless mobs rushing toward the mountain on the west. As he did, for a split second, he rushed into a fog, and when he did, his mind cleared. He skidded to a stop and realized he was in a tiny radiation haze produced by a local material called terpalian. He stood stock still and realized everyone not in that tiny haze patch was still under the control of the madness.

"It took him three months of work, night and day, to figure out how to produce it on a large scale and centralize it over the valley. He used every ounce of the substance that could be found on the planet, which was not too hard since it is localized to this area. He did not ask a single soul for permission; he knew the trouble it would cause. He just did it. When he fired it up, it took just an hour for the valley to be covered in the haze. Everyone's mind cleared instantly.

"It was then that he stepped forward and told everyone what danger they were facing and what he had done to stop it. That was many, many years ago, and no one has left the valley since."

"Athaga, ewet moya dopar."

"No, D, it isn't good, and we can't leave. You and I have seen what these people call terpalian before. We call it druidirium. When energized, it has a fairly short half-life. Based on my calculations as to when all of this began, that

115

barrier has only a few days left until it dissipates completely."

After a few seconds of utter silence, Deragon spoke again.

"Lina eimi ewet tezer ut rosem?"

"Well, what do we know? What are the facts we have to work with?"

The next few minutes were a confusing jumble of points, counterpoints, and beneficial arguments. They went over everything from the time they were first contacted by Andromeda until now with a fine tooth comb. Finally, these facts could be agreed upon.

One: the range of these creatures' power was long, but not limitless.

Two: Andromeda was the stronger of the two in her influence.

Three: having the two of them in the same place made things infinitely worse.

Four: once the barrier was gone, these helpless and hapless valley dwellers would be easy prey.

Five: the mind benders in the hills clearly could not or would not cross the barrier, or they would already have done so to regain their control over their "subjects."

Six: the only ones remotely capable of dealing with these two were Zak and Deragon.

Seven: the only way even they could do anything was to somehow utilize the terpalian to do so.

Eight: the only terpalian available was right there in the valley.

So I suppose it is only natural that they decided to steal it.

CHAPTER TWENTY

By the time the suns rose over the valley, Zak and Deragon were sitting under a tree on a hill right near the barrier, looking down over the city.

"This has got to be perfect, D, we cannot afford a single mistake. We could try to explain everything to them, but you and I both know they would never, ever understand it. If we just fly away, in a matter of days they will be done for, and for some reason, I cannot live with that."

Deragon just sat silently, looking at his friend, watching while he rubbed his chin in contemplation. What was happening to Zak Blue? True, he was about to steal a valuable substance, but only so that he could save the people that had it. Such a complication, such a contradiction from one who had always lived by one rule: always look out for number one.

"Once we get it, all Gehenna is going to break loose, as the ancients used to say. The

119

people in the city, as simple minded as they are, are still going to realize that they are at risk and that we are the ones who caused it. The mind benders are going to realize that they have access to mess with minds again, and they will quickly do so.

"My hope is that so many people to mess with all at once, after years of being denied access, will be an overload for them, and they won't see us coming."

Deragon stood up over his friend and started warbling angrily and waving his arms.

"No, D, I don't want to do that. I admit, it would be the easiest course, just contacting Falcon Wing and having her destroy them both. But I think you and I both know that people often become what they become because of what people put them through. Maybe those trouble making mind bender creatures are not so very different from a couple of other trouble makers we know.

"So, what if we could create a situation in which no one really loses?"

Deragon whistled again, this time more angrily than ever.

Laughing, Zak answered his agitated friend. "Who am I, and what have I done with the real Zak Blue? Seriously?"

Zak stood up slowly and put his arms on his smaller friend's scaly shoulders.

"D, for whatever reason, you have always trusted me. You ask who I am? I am not really sure anymore, other than to say that I am still Zak

Blue, but maybe just a bit more thoughtful than before. Trust me now like you always have before."

Deragon breathed heavily and slowly, gills opening widely and then closing again. Finally, he dropped his head a bit to the right, looked crookedly upward at his friend, and made up his mind.

"O pistos oyt."

Zak smiled. "Good, very good." Now let's make some plans.

Having been in and out of the haze a couple of times, Zak knew that it was like every other haze in one regard. It behaved much like a very light liquid; it flowed in a very logical and predictable rounded wave.

Retrieving a mini drone once again, Zak squeezed it and spoke.

"Zak Bluetoo, I have a job for you."

Instantly Zak's digital alter ego was projected in front of him once again. "What can I do for you, my criminal cohort?"

"Go to three hundred feet. Analyze the wave pattern of the haze, and tell me where the very center of it comes from."

Instantly the drone shot upward. In a matter of seconds, Zak Bluetoo reappeared.

"Easy find, that one. Dead center of the valley. If you like, I will be a little lightning bug, and you can follow me right to it."

"I would like," Zak smiled, "but not quite yet. With the suns up, people will be milling about. This will have to be a night-time escapade."

That began a mixed emotion kind of a day for Zak and Deragon. They stayed far out of the city and out of sight since they did not even want it to be known that they were still in the valley. In other words, they had nothing to do, and no one telling them what to do, freedom and boredom.

Soon enough, though, the first sun kissed the horizon and then dipped behind it, cutting the light under the haze significantly. It was followed a few moments later by the second sun making its trek below the line, which turned the light off completely.

With nary a word, Zak and Deragon rose, Zak activated his little firefly, and they began to make their way down into the city.

As they wound their way down quiet lane after quiet lane, they finally made a left turn and found themselves in the very heart of the town, the center of the valley. And yet, having achieved their immediate goal, their reaction was not the least bit celebratory.

Perhaps that was because, the center of the town was a four-sided wall, a stone box fully thirty feet high on all sides, with no opening whatsoever.

122

"Lina imdea?"

"Good question," Zak whispered back. "Clearly, these folks wanted to make sure that no one, ever, could mess with the source of the haze, not even themselves. Out of sight, out of mind, out of memory. Sadly, for them, they do not know that their precious protection against the madness is not eternal."

If they had been at the Falcon Wing, they could have gone to the engineering room and in a matter of moments been holding energon hover boards. But, since that was not an option and times was drifting away fast, they would have to be much more "old school" on this one.

"Problem solving 101. We need to get inside, get the terpalian, and then get back out. Thirty feet walls. Very smooth surface. Three possible options; over, under, or through. We have no shovel, nor do I really want to break a sweat digging, so under is out. We cannot get through without making a lot of noise, so through is out. Our only option is over.

"That brings us to the means of over. They are as follows: pushed upward from below, as in a jump or a ladder or being projected forcibly upward, pulled from above, as in someone up there with a rope hauling us up, or lifted up, like in an old-fashioned hot air balloon."

As he said it, his eyes grew wide, and the picture began to take shape in his mind. Whirling around like a shot, he ran back up the street, with D in hot pursuit. Three blocks down, a sharp right, four blocks up, a left, then a skid to a stop in front of a fabric shop that Zak had noticed on their first day here.

"Somehow, it's always like this, isn't it? I am about to break, enter, and steal, and if I don't, these people may well kill each other. Well, no need wringing my hands and putting myself under conviction I guess."

It took Zak less than seven seconds to pick the utterly simplistic lock. A few minutes later he and Deragon were shutting the door carefully behind them, locking it back and rushing back to the center of town. Zak was focused on the task, but Deragon was divided in his thinking.

It had not escaped his notice that, just before they left the fabric shop, Zak had left one of his prized possessions behind; an old silver coin that he always kept for good luck. Would it be of any value here? Deragon wasn't sure.

What he was sure was that it meant the world to Zak.

CHAPTER TWENTY-ONE

Back at the box in the center of town, Zak furiously set to work. His genius mind and nimble hands soon had a rudimentary balloon and cords fashioned. Not huge, but hopefully big enough.

"Okay, D, here is the thing. You are lighter than my one seventy by a good thirty pounds, so you get to be the guinea pig; this will carry your weight, but not mine, its max capacity is one-fifty. Strap these loops under your arms. Once they are in place, take your energon clip, and slowly open it into the fabric. It will heat the air just like a fire would, and if my calculations are correct, and they always are, you are going to be able to float slowly up, over the wall, and then down into the center as you pull the energon clip back just a bit."

Deragon shook his head in bewilderment.

"Hefa gi oya skema?"

"Yeah, buddy, that is my plan. Got a better one?"

The Tarq put a hand on either side of his head and shook it side to side as he scrunched his eyes up. As always, he could not decide if he was more bothered by how foolish Zak's plan was, or by the fact that he could not seem to come up with a better one.

A few moments later, his scaly feet were off of the ground. His legs were flailing as he tried to steady himself.

"Easy, D, easy!" Zak hissed. "Relax!"

Deragon took a deep breath and loosened up, foot by foot he got farther and farther from the ground until his head popped up over the top of the wall. With a little wiggling and flailing and adjusting of the energon clip, he made his way over the lip of the wall and started descending down into the center. It dawned on him then that he had no idea what to expect when he got down to the bottom!

Fortunately, for once, things did not end in some disaster, predictable or otherwise. There, in the center of the box, was an utterly brilliant yet simple arrangement. About ten pounds of terpalian, druidirium, boxed in by thin magnetic sheets and focused upwards in waves by a Coridium Refractor. The entire arrangement, this beautiful, elegant, madness inhibiting system, would weigh no more than forty pounds.

Which, if you have a good memory and some decent math ability, you will realize was thirty pounds too much.

As Deragon realized the problem, he nearly beat his head against the wall in frustration. He let out a series of angry whistles and warbles, which Zak could just barely hear from the outside.

"What, D, what's going on?" he hissed.

Inside the box, Deragon tapped the side of his temple activating his implanted com. The next sixty seconds was a mixture of him explaining the problem and insulting his best friend, whom he was, in fact, very angry with at the moment.

Zak grimaced and slumped down beside the wall. How could he have missed that? Worse, how could he ever get Deragon to go along with the only possible solution? Slowly, he tapped the side of his own temple and spoke in a very measured tone.

"Buddy, you aren't going to like this but hear me out. We have to get both you and the haze maker out of there, but we can only do that one at a time and, sadly, it can't get you out, but you can get it out. I need you to trust me. Hook everything up to the balloon, heat it up enough for it to float out, and I will go get it, wherever it lands. Then I will come back for you."

Deragon could not believe what he was hearing. Stunned, he began to make noises that our language really doesn't have words for. They were not trills or whistles or burbs of beeps, they were just sounds that Zak knew were saved only for the times of the greatest of Tarq anger and incredulity.

Deragon had known Zak for a long time, at least for a long time as far as their relative youth was concerned. He was being asked to send his only means of escape floating up out of the hole and trust the most selfish person he had ever known to come back for him.

He remembered all of the lies Zak had told in his nearly seventeen years of life, all of the things he had stolen, all of the times he said something while crossing his fingers, never intending to follow through.

But he also remembered a silver coin left on a counter just a few moments before.

Maybe that is why Zak soon saw a cloth balloon floating out of the box and drifting over the town.

Lots of things began to happen all at once. The haze began to lift as the balloon lifted, and as it drifted north across the town (at a faster rate than Zak had anticipated), the barrier began to drift north with it.

Instantly Zak was up and running. He came to the face of a building, grabbed a

128

downspout, and used it to climb up like a spider. Once he was onto the roof, he set off on a dead run, leaping from on rooftop to another in hot pursuit of the mini hot air balloon. Man, that thing was moving! He knew he should have taken the stiff breeze into account on this part.

The balloon was pulling away, and Zak realized in horror that he was running out of rooftops.

The ancients used to talk about horses "pinning their ears back" when they ran. Zak did so now, putting every ounce of energy in his body into catching that balloon. Five rooftops left, leap...four, leap...three, leap...two, leap...one, leap...none, and yet one more leap anyway.

CHAPTER TWENTY-TWO

There is a moment of weightlessness, at least it feels like such, when you jump off into nothingness. Zak felt that now, but with no euphoria. Every fiber of his being was focused on stretching just as far as he could...as he snagged a cord of the balloon.

Three seconds later he was landing, hard, onto the dusty cobblestone street. Fortunately, he was unhurt, but he knew his battle was just beginning. He was at least twenty blocks away from the box and Deragon, the valley was now largely exposed on the southern side, and those angry bells beginning to ring told him that someone on the valley now realized there was a problem and was sounding the alarm.

He could not go back for his best friend.

He had to get out of town as fast as he could.

Zak bolted toward the nearest side of The Valley, weighed down by everything he was carrying. His legs were aching, his lungs were burning, and his mind was racing. This was not working at all like he had hoped. Why, oh why had he and D not just flown away and left all of this horrid mess behind? Was it not enough that all of Planetary Command was chasing him across the universe? Did he really have to go and put himself in a situation where angry Ryannis were going to be after him as well? And if they didn't get him, the mind benders surely would, unless he could strike quickly.

Zak, he thought to himself as he ran, *you are a blithering idiot. You could be cruising the universe, and yet here you are, getting your goodie-two-shoes self into a jam you will never get out of. Tiller Mansen isn't your problem, you are.*

Once he cleared the valley, he spoke rapidly into his com. "Falcon Wing, this is Captain Blue. Come to my location immediately, full stealth mode, not a sight or a sound at all."

In the cockpit, the Falcon Wing came to life.

"Aye aye, captain, I will be at your location in forty-nine seconds."

Back in the town, as Zak suspected, all Gehenna was indeed breaking loose. The townspeople were lighting torches, rushing out into the street, and pointing upward at the clear skies and bright stars.

"The barrier!" one cried, "it's gone! Someone has destroyed the barrier! What is the meaning of this?"

Naturally, everyone began shouting and arguing all at once, producing an unintelligible cacophony. But just as naturally, it did not take people long at all to focus their attention on the only obvious source, Zak and Deragon.

"They were asking about the barrier!" Mr. Bear shouted gruffly. "They did it! We must find them; they must pay for what they have done!"

In the box, Deragon was utterly silent, not wanting to be found, and utterly angry, not wanting to believe that Zak had left him behind.

Zak was now inside Falcon Wing and was rapidly climbing. His chute was ready; this would be an old fashioned halo jump. This had to work, it just had to, and it had to work fast.

Once Falcon Wing was 20,000 feet over Castella's lair, Zak barked the order, the jump hatch popped open, and he dove out.

At 2,000 feet, Zak pulled the ripcord, and the chute popped open.

Fifteen seconds later he landed in the dirt, a perfect strike, right outside Castella's cave. Hearing the thud, she jumped up from sleep, looked toward the entry of the cave and saw Zak Blue flip the switch on the barrier maker.

Her eyes grew wide, but by the time she could think of a thought to plant in his mind, it was too late. She was trapped in her cave, and Zak Blue was gone.

Seconds later, Zak was back in the Falcon Wing, heading back to their original location on this now hated planet called Velaronas Four. He still had one more mind bender to deal with.

CHAPTER TWENTY-THREE

By the time the sun was up, Klingscleft was in a tizzy. Everyone knew the barrier was gone, and everyone was in a panic. The older ones were weeping; they had experienced the madness before. The younger ones, for the most part, were just confused. If they were upset, it was only because the adults were upset.

Sybillia, sweet Sybillia, seemed utterly matter-of-fact about the whole thing.

"I don't think we ought to worry until we have something to worry about. And if we have something we know to worry about, we will know what it is, so we probably won't have to worry anyway."

Inside the box, Deragon could hear her shouting those words above the din of the frightened masses, and he chuckled to himself. True, he had been abandoned by his friend, but at least this world would be a rather entertaining sort of boring/madness, at least as long as this kid was around.

That was about as far as he got in his musings because he suddenly felt a warm energy that could only mean one thing...

A moment later he realized he was right, as he found himself sitting in the co-pilot seat of the Falcon Wing.

"Welcome back, buddy, you didn't think I had left without you, did you?"

Deragon cocked his head and raised one eyebrow on his scaly face, and said nothing.

"Yeah, I thought so. But just hold that thought, we have some loose ends to tie up here."

Zak stepped into the center of the bridge and gave a command.

"Falcon Wing, project me into the center of the town and give me eyes there as well."

A second later, the entire cockpit appeared to be the town center, complete with all of the perplexed, angry people. For their part, the people in the town were stunned into silence by a hologram of Zak Blue suddenly standing in their midst.

"Good people of The Valley" and as he said this he smiled and nodded at Sybillia, "and of the town of Klingscleft. I apologize for causing such a stir. You will not understand all of it, but please know that we did all we did because, whether you know it or not, you needed us to.

"We are going to be leaving now, and it is not likely that you will ever see us again.

136

Please know that you will always hold a very special place in our hearts as you were the first stop along the way in our great space chase.

"You do not know it yet, but you need never fear the mind benders or the madness again. The barrier is now in place over the opening of a cave. As the opening is so much smaller than the valley itself, it will last for many generations there.

"You also do not know this: you have in your midst a future leader of your people. When she grows up, put Sybillia in charge. If you do, I doubt seriously if you will ever have any serious problems ever again.

"Farewell, be safe, thank you for the stibble fruit, and we will think of you kindly for many years to come, assuming we live that long."

And with that, the hologram of Zak Blue disappeared, and the Falcon Wing made her way out into space to continue her journey to who knows where.

CHAPTER TWENTY-FOUR

As Zak and Deragon watched Velaronas Four fade from view, Deragon was very quiet. He was not sure anymore how to regard his friend. True, he left him, but he did come back for him. They were safe, the nightmare of their first stop was behind them, and the sensors showed no sign of pursuit from Planetary Command.

"Hefa ebatsa gleemuth, dolnen da blockut asa hefa."

"I don't know if I would go so far as to call it brilliant, but, yeah, I guess it was pretty smart. She is alive, Sybillia will no doubt make sure people toss food and water into her, but she won't be able to cause any harm. I guess jail is better than death."

As he said it, it hit him...

"Except for me, of course."

139

Deragon looked over at him again, and barked one simple word: "weldo."

"Right, us. Well, like the ancients said, 'all's well that ends well.' "

There are those moments when something hits you, something so unbelievably huge and obvious that it is just jaw dropping. Deragon suddenly had one of those moments.

"Lina torva Andromeda?"

"Andromeda? Oh, uh, yeah, about that..."

To be continued in volume two, <u>Enter the Maelstrom.</u>